THE
BENEVOLENT
TERRORIST

A Novel By

Danny Wynn

Bright Lights Big City Books

The Benevolent Terrorist
Copyright © 2016 Danny Wynn
Published by Bright Lights Big City Books

Printed in the United States of America
First Edition Printing

Design by
Arbor Services, Inc.
http://www.arborservices.co/

Editing by
Martha Hughes, Julie Mosow, Lucy Kaylin, and Pam Nordberg

ISBN: 978-0-692-78345-0
LCCN: 2016915568

1. Title   2. Author   3. Fiction

Also by Danny Wynn:

Man from the Sky, a novella
Lucien And I, a collage novel

For my mother

CHAPTER 1

Mid-August 1989.

Jack and Jenkins motored across the Aegean in an aluminum twenty-footer as the sun broke the horizon, the water choppy, wind whipping. The legendary Aegean, which Jack had first read about at age fifteen as a place of rare grandeur and dreamed of sailing on. He'd lived his dream by the time he was eighteen. Now he was twenty-eight, an American wandering the world in an increasingly futile search for something worth doing.

They were headed for a private island—one villa only—where the man they sought was reportedly staying. Jenkins manned the tiller of the outboard motor. His duffel bag lay next to him on the bottom of the boat, containing an M16 and Browning semi-automatic, both fully loaded, along with a half dozen extra magazines of ammo for each.

Jack sat in the prow, catching blasts of spray on his face and T-shirt, feeling rugged. Fated and doomed—the type of feeling he'd romanticized for so much of his life. He'd had similar sensations in the past, but they'd always seemed a bit contrived, like walking in the rain by yourself to more purely experience a feeling of sadness. This time, however, his somber but stirring mood felt deserved, coming from somewhere deep within.

He felt like he was about to do the first real thing in his life.

1

Trailing behind, attached by a nylon rope, was a small rowboat bouncing over the waves. Jack hadn't looked back since they'd left Kyros, another of the Greek isles, but he knew the shadow people were sitting silently on the rowboat's benches, in their monk-like robes with oversized hoods, their corporeal substance somehow gray and translucent at the same time.

He never came close to asking Jenkins why he'd come. The exploit had begun. It was going to happen. Or something was.

* * *

Two months earlier. Athens.

Mornings really are the worst times, thought Jack, tired to his core. He sat naked on the edge of his single bed in the seedy hotel room, feet on the linoleum floor, elbows on his knees, leaden head buried in his hands, waiting for the communal bathroom down the hall to free up. The bothersome tooth in the upper right side of his jaw felt like it was being jabbed violently with a sharp tool. *God, it hurts.* It was almost noon. Timmy had already gone out. Her bed was neatly made—not by the maids, whose service was sporadic at best. He and Timmy hadn't run across one another awake in almost three days. He thought about doing a line but decided to try to do without.

The problem with mornings is they mean another day. Christ. He grimaced. *How hokey can I get?*

He was in the depths of a crushing speed crash, combined with a run-of-the-mill hangover, and was about as depressed as he'd ever been, though that would be going some. The dreary room had only one window, overlooking a refuse-strewn area between buildings, and felt unbearably stuffy.

They really are the worst, though. Mornings make you face things. Make it difficult to ignore the obvious.

He heard the door down the hall open and shut, and stood up, which took just about everything he had in him.

Forty-five minutes later, he stepped gingerly out the front door of the boardinghouse onto a dirty street. The brightness and heat hit him like a blow. He winced, almost reeled. Stepping back inside, he fumbled in his knapsack for his broken sunglasses. Outside for another try, he walked slowly down a side street toward the noise and turmoil of the hectic city.

It was hot as hell, had to be close to a hundred. *It's early June*, he thought. *This is just plain wrong.* He stopped about fifty feet short of a bustling traffic circle and leaned against a shaded wall, breathing too hard for the exertion he'd made so far. He literally hurt, all over. *The goddamn speed.* The night before, he'd soared, every intake of breath supercharging him with power and exhilaration. Later, though, he'd nosedived, engines screaming, and crashed violently into the rocks of reality. He was shattered by the loss of the glorious high and return to regular life. He felt the urge to cry, which he hadn't done in years, but tears were nowhere near his surface, if anywhere inside him at all.

On top of everything else, the toothache that had started a week before was throbbing at a new level of excruciating. The last thing he wanted to do was find a dentist.

Jesus, Greece isn't working for me the way it used to. Where's the solace I used to get from just being here?

The intensity of feeling subsided and he resumed walking. Emerged onto a large roundabout with hundreds of little cars whizzing by, along with vans and small trucks. Lowering his sunglasses slightly, he could almost see the particles of haze hanging in the air, a combination of dust and smog. The surrounding buildings were all squat and various shades of off-white.

He walked over to a kiosk and bought a *Tribune*. Thought about where to go for some badly needed coffee. He knew of a square nearby with outdoor cafés, but they'd be full of tourists and he wasn't in the mood for that, not to mention sitting outside in the heat, even under an awning in the shade. He wasn't usually this fragile. He had a surprisingly strong constitution, notwithstanding his skinny, scraggly appearance, which was what enabled him to endure all that he endured.

Timmy might be at work. She'd found a job waitressing at a bar— illegal since she was a foreigner, Australian, but she was a pretty blond and the manager had overlooked the issue. The Greeks always seemed to find a way around the system when it suited them. She mostly worked nights, though, and there didn't seem to be much point to their contact these days.

He walked, letting his mind drift. *What an ugly city.* Most of the buildings were completely utilitarian, reflecting no aesthetic considerations at all. They weren't old but already looked rundown. Everything was dirty—the walls of the buildings, the streets, empty lots with scattered trash. The relentless noise and harshness. *Christ, this is the cradle of Western Civilization?*

He had a flash, unconnected to anything, of deliberately taking aim with a heavy handgun and squeezing the trigger, the blast reverberating through his arm and body.

He saw a plain-looking restaurant among a row of shops; it would have been called a coffee shop back in New York, run by Greeks there as well. The lighting inside didn't look too bright to deal with, and he went in. *Air conditioning, thank the Lord.* Not producing much cooling, but a lot better than nothing. A couple of middle-aged guys sat at a table in the back smoking foul-smelling cigarettes and jabbering in Greek. They had coffee cups in front of them and might have been customers, but they had an air of spending a lot of time where they sat, and more likely were management. The only other people in the place were a waiter and a short-order cook with a permanent-looking scowl. Jack sat at a table in front and ordered coffee, orange juice, and water, feeling limp, not ready for solid food yet. He thought about going back to the hotel and doing some meth. That would certainly fix the state he was in, but then there would be what to do when that wore off. He could just take more, of course—he still had a fair-sized supply—a pattern of use he'd fallen into too many times to remember. But as people said, speed kills. And before that, it makes you psychotic, never a good thing. Besides, the thought of the crash that would follow another extended binge was enough to put the fears in him. The for-real fears. The feral fears.

He'd read about a guy once, a prominent intellectual, who'd tripped on LSD for three straight weeks, and after the inevitable crash said, "It was as if I'd been let into the kingdom of heaven, and then made to leave."

It was amazing what you could carry through customs in prescription medicine bottles. He'd returned to the States four months earlier for the sole purpose of replenishment. He'd flown from Hong Kong to LAX, and on arrival gone to the nearest Barclays Bank and withdrawn seven thousand dollars. Then to a CVS where he bought large quantities of over-the-counter medicines for headaches, colds, and allergies, in capsule form. The gum-chewing Hispanic cashier didn't even glance at him as she rang up his dubious purchase.

He returned to LAX and flew to Midland, Texas. There, pursuant to an arrangement that had been a major pain in the ass to make from Asia, he took a three-minute taxi ride to the Belmont Inn next to the small airport, walked up a flight of outdoor stairs and along an open walkway to room 223, and knocked. The door opened to reveal a sawed-off double-barreled shotgun pointed squarely at his chest, held by a man with long dark hair wearing a red and black patterned bandana on his head. He had some Indian blood in him and eyes that were either crazed or empty, it was hard to tell which. Jack strangely had the presence of mind to think that eyes with either of those qualities should look distinctly different than the other kind, and he was at a loss to understand why he couldn't tell which kind these ones were.

"It's cool, it's cool," he said shakily. "It's me, Jack Ferris. Please lower the gun." The guy started to, but then snapped it back up. Jack flinched and felt some urine dribble into his underwear. The guy laughed harshly and tossed the gun on the bed; Jack half expected it to go off when it landed. The left side of the guy's face had a bad twitch. They made their exchange, and Jack left.

He took a taxi to the Doubletree Hotel, a generic establishment devoid of all shadiness, and checked in under the name Jim Carroll, using a phony-looking fake ID. In his room, he emptied several hundred capsules of over-the-counter medicines and refilled them with methamphetamine powder. Put the capsules into prescription medicine bottles with labels identifying them as various common tranquilizers, mood elevators, and muscle relaxants. He then went to the airport and flew back to Hong Kong via LAX.

The waiter brought Jack's liquids, and he began to sip the coffee and skim the *Tribune* listlessly. His eye was caught by an article about one of the most expensive parties of all time, recently thrown in Deauville over a four-day period, including a polo tournament. But the effort of reading beyond the first couple of paragraphs was too much, and who the fuck cared anyway?

As his mind went slack, the question began to inexorably form in his thoughts—*what am I doing here?* Lately, not a day went by when it didn't occur to him at least a dozen times. Sometimes there were slight variations like, *What the fuck am I doing?* or *What am I gonna do?* They were not so much questions as insistent demands that he make some minimal effort to deal with the current state of himself and his life. Sometimes he managed to come up with a vague sense of how things were going with him, how he'd gotten in his present situation. Once in a while, he actually succeeded in thinking with focus about his plight, and grappled with various decisions looming in front of him, factors that might be relevant. On rare occasion, he even thought he'd figured out a thing or two, but knew he could easily be fooling himself. Other times, he just got angry and whipped himself with caustic thoughts, feeling like a penitent self-flagellating monk. Mostly, though, he just let his mind float over and around the questions and his predicament, getting some masochistic pleasure out of dwelling on it all and feeling sorry for himself. After all, two of his defining characteristics, as he was all too well aware, were his tenacious self-pity and stylized despair.

Except for the replenishment trip, he'd been away from the States on his current round of world travel for over nine months, which in some ways was more responsible for his condition than the speed. Traveling long term took it out of you big time, especially doing it on the cheap. This was the fourth time he'd been out wandering the planet for an extended time. Money-wise, he was able to do it, as well as lead his dabbling undisciplined life in general, because of a trust fund established by a long-dead grandfather he'd never met, which provided him with about $40,000 "per annum"—not enough to be extravagant but enough to get by on and avoid working. Recently he'd been allowed to start invading the principal, and between that and inflation, he knew the bequest wasn't going to last forever. But it was unclear how long "forever" was going to be in his case.

His parents had died in a car crash when he was twelve, and it turned out they'd been living on fumes for their last few years, having exhausted the considerable wealth they'd previously enjoyed, though enjoy probably wasn't the right word in light of how little happiness they'd manifested.

This morning, though, he just felt too shitty to beat himself up or search for answers. And it was so boring. He turned to the international classifieds and skimmed them, looking for offbeat items, reading for no particular reason about houses and apartments for sale or rent in posh locales—villas in Tuscany, flats in Knightsbridge, et cetera. He saw a legal notice making a certainly ineffectual attempt to inform "an Italian male in his mid-twenties named Massimo" that he'd fathered a child the summer before on the island of Capri, and there were proceedings going on in Minnesota to eliminate his parental rights. Jack pondered that one for several moments. The front door of the restaurant opened and someone walked in.

A guy, not Greek, maybe northern European, about forty, six feet, solid-looking but with a bit of a paunch. He had close-cropped brown hair, a crude-looking face with shallow pockmarks, and a full mustache. Jack had never gotten mustaches, but this one at least seemed to suit the guy, who glanced around and took a table next to a wall. He gave off the distinct vibe of someone you didn't want to mess with, the kind of guy who could make people uncomfortable just by being in the same room with them. He glanced at the menu and ordered with an American accent—scrambled eggs, bacon, and coffee. He took a red and white pack of cigarettes from his shirt pocket and lit one. Smoke curled in the air above him.

Jack wondered what his story was. *Doesn't look like a tourist.* Jack had the impulse to talk to him, despite his intimidating quality. It might relieve things a bit to have some conversation. And one of his objectives in drifting around the world was supposed to be experiencing different

kinds of people. He had vague notions of writing some things down one
of these years.

He sipped his coffee for another minute or so, producing an internal
urge. He got up and went into the *banyo*. It was cleaner than most of
the bathrooms he'd been in over the past several months. He prodded
his problem tooth with his finger, triggering a sharp jab of pain, almost
producing the tears that wouldn't come earlier. He took his first crap
in several days, which required a sustained effort. Turned on the tap
indicating cold, and splashed lukewarm water on his face repeatedly,
kneading his skin roughly with his fingers. No towels. *As usual.* He
used the bottom of his T-shirt, white with "Faded Glory" printed on
the front, to reduce his dripping face to moistness. He went back out,
feeling a bit better.

To his surprise, the guy was gone, apparently not a leisurely eater. Jack
was mildly disappointed but wasn't sure he'd have mustered the psychic
energy to talk to him anyway.

———————

Standing on the sidewalk outside, Jack was at a loss as to what to do. It
seemed hotter than ever. It was way too early in the year for heat like this.
He'd read in the *Trib* awhile back about Isaac Asimov giving a speech
about the "greenhouse effect." And more recently, he'd read of an official
at the UN saying that within ten years, "global warming" could result in
entire nations being submerged by rising sea levels. Maybe these guys
were onto something.

He didn't know anybody in Athens other than Timmy. He used to know a rich Greek kid back in New York who lived in a four-story townhouse on his own—speedballs were his drug cocktail of choice— and he also had an apartment in Athens, but Jack hadn't kept in touch and wouldn't know how to begin tracking him down even if he could be bothered. Sightseeing didn't come close to crossing his mind. And he definitely didn't want to sit at a café. He'd done a ridiculous amount of the café thing in the course of his extended meandering. He had a fleeting thought of returning to the boardinghouse and packing his bag, catching a taxi to the airport, and flying somewhere. Or more appealing, having the driver take him to Piraeus and boarding a ferry to one of the islands that for a long time had epitomized the idyllic life for him. But he hadn't planned on moving on for a few days yet, and besides he'd have to figure out where to go.

He stood on the pavement immobilized, sinking into a kind of stupor that lasted maybe two or three minutes. Then he roused himself and headed for the bar where Timmy worked.

It was in the back part of the Plaka, where the labyrinth of crooked little streets still had some authentic character. It took him about fifteen minutes to walk there. Inside the bar, he didn't see her. There was a smattering of customers. To his relief, she emerged through a door in the back. She saw him but was busy and didn't react, taking a rack of dirty glasses into the back. He sat down on a stool by the wall and rested one arm on a narrow drink shelf.

When she came back out, she walked over to him, wiping her hands on her apron. She was twenty-six. Not drop-dead beautiful, but very pretty.

Her most striking feature was a lion's mane of wavy blond hair hanging down around her shoulders. And a close second were her china-blue eyes that made Jack think of cool breezes on a hot day when he was feeling maudlin. She had a lovely tan, which went nicely with her golden ringlets. Her figure was slender and leggy, calling to mind a graceful colt. She usually wore skimpy, loose-fitting clothing, though he'd only seen her in hot places. He'd met her in the Seychelles a few months back, and they'd been traveling together since.

"Hi," she said in a flat tone.

"Hi," he said awkwardly.

She waited.

He tried to think of something to say and was about to try "How're you doing?" when she said in her broad Australian accent, "You look bloody awful."

He considered different responses for a few seconds, then shrugged. "Yeah, well, these things happen." He looked around. "How're things going with you?"

"Okay." She smiled. "This place is all right. The boss keeps his hands to himself, and it's usually fun later on. Too many Germans some nights."

He remembered she was basically a happy person. In the course of their travels, he'd caught a hint of sadness in her once in a while, but it always passed quickly.

"You want anything?" she asked. "Coffee? Water?"

"Uh, you got any hash?"

She looked at him for a moment or two, then said, "You oughta lay off the drugs awhile."

A dark cloud flooded his brain. He didn't want to hear it. He stared out the open door for a few moments, letting the cloud pass. He thought about asking her to sit down with him and talk for a few minutes, not about anything in particular, just to have some human contact. But he knew she wouldn't.

"Seriously, Tim, you got any hash?"

Despite his many horrible qualities, he'd always been generous with her in non-emotional ways, and she wasn't the "brother's keeper" type. With a frown, she went into the kitchen,. Came back out a minute later, and slipped him a folded-up napkin.

"Thanks. Got a cigarette?"

She gave him one.

"I've been thinking about moving on." He hadn't planned on saying it before he did.

"Yeah?" she said with the tough manner she sometimes assumed. "Where to?"

"Uh, don't know. I'll figure it out over the next day or so." Somebody at the bar knocked a glass to the floor; it bounced loudly but didn't break. "I'll see you back at the room. Or maybe here later on."

Before he left, he went into the bathroom, took a rolling paper from his knapsack and creased it, crumbled some of the hash, tore the cigarette open, mixed the crumbs and tobacco shreds in the fold. And rolled a joint.

———————————

He walked to a small plaza shaped like a half moon that served as a back entrance to the Plaka, the ancient neighborhood next to the Acropolis filled with touristy shops, bars, and tavernas. Narrow streets and alleys led like spokes from the semicircle into the mazelike district.

Jack sat down on some stone steps on one side of the *piazza*. Lots of people were walking by and milling around. Most of the cafés and shops were open, not always the case during a sweltering mid-afternoon. He looked about to make sure no one was paying attention, then lit his joint. It was an exceptionally stupid thing to do. Greece was not a drug-tolerant country. But stupid things were one of Jack's specialties. The tobacco smell partly disguised the odor of the hash, and he only took two quick hits before stubbing out the joint and putting it in the back pocket of his tattered jeans. The sweet taste of the hash gave him some immediate Pavlovian relief from his free-floating anxiety, and the high from the THC soon followed, spreading smoothly through his system and taking the edge off things more distinctly. He sat back and gazed at the scene in front of him. This was something he did well—hanging out and watching the parade go by.

The pain in his tooth had subsided some, *thank God*.

He thought about how he'd lost so much of his enjoyment of traveling. The first several times he'd gone to a foreign country, in his late teens, everything had been ultra-fresh-and-vivid, even the most mundane details, as if he'd regained his child eyes and was seeing things for the first time. It had felt great to just do simple, ordinary things like walk down a street or eat in a restaurant, and be fully absorbed, easily, consistently. He thought he'd made a brilliant discovery as to how to keep life interesting.

At the time, he'd begun to realize that most entertainments and diversions got old sooner or later—music, movies, drugs, clubbing, chasing women, et cetera. You could only go to the well so often. But travel struck him as something that wouldn't go stale, would stay engaging for a lifetime, because there would always be new places to go, places that would give him his child eyes again.

But he'd been wrong. For one thing, over the years he'd managed to go to an awful lot of places. He'd done the basics in Europe and the Med, moved onto Southeast Asia, India, Nepal, down under, a number of island paradises. A bit of the Middle East and Africa. On an earlier expedition, he'd drifted around South America for several months, partly on a motorcycle, like Che at around the same age.

He never rushed. He had time and enjoyed immersing himself in a locale, getting the feel of its rhythms, discovering places off the beaten track, hangout venues he'd have frequented if he were a local. He stayed a month or longer, sometimes three or four, in each of Cadaques, Amsterdam, Punta Del Este, Goa, Koh Samui, and Sydney. And he spent a semester in London, making a second unsuccessful stab at university. He'd never been drawn to explore the US. It seemed so plain and dull.

And for another thing, he discovered that just because there were always new places to go didn't mean the new place would always be fresh and vibrant. Arriving in an untried foreign place for the fiftieth time wasn't the same as arriving in a place like that for the first several dazzling mind-expanding times. It still had some newness, but the experience had taken on a routine quality as well.

And of course there was the old trite-but-truism—no matter where you go, there you are. An exceptionally unfortunate phenomenon in Jack's case.

So, traveling, like so many other interesting pastimes, had lost a big part of its pizzazz.

And here he was, sitting on some outdoor steps in Athens as the sun went to hell, overdosed on the road and foreign lands. The obvious thought was to go back to New York and try to establish some kind of regular life there. But he'd tried that a number of times already.

Well, he mused, *another useful day winds down in the grand annals of aimlessness.*

CHAPTER 2

Jenkins looked through the binoculars, studying the modern white villa about a mile away, at the base of a promontory, partly hidden by trees. He and Jack were drifting slightly, the outboard motor off for the last half hour. Jenkins had first directed the field glasses at the other end of the modest-sized island to focus them, and then turned toward the residence holding them by the front, his hands cupped over the forward lenses to prevent any glint. It was around eleven in the morning; the day was already another scorcher in what had been an extraordinarily hot summer. Jenkins lowered the binoculars for a moment, made a slight adjustment, then resumed his surveillance.

The two men hadn't spoken for the last twenty minutes or so. Before that, Jenkins had talked steadily—quietly, insistently—giving Jack revised instructions dealing with the last-minute change of plans.

As they floated on the glittering sea, Jack lay down on the front bench, resting his head on a life vest he placed over the gunwale. For some reason, the life jackets seemed like useless orange objects to him. The waves rocked him gently as he stared up at the saturated cobalt sky.

Something, he didn't know what, prompted him to sit up and look at the rectangular white house in the distance. An eerie sensation of acute lucidity came over him, as if his mind were more sharp and clear than it had ever been. For a few moments, he felt as if he understood everything—life, the world, himself, the human condition. It all seemed evident and coherent, as if there were a globe of the earth floating in the air in front of him, intricately detailed, with curious mechanisms attached to the surface and transparent tubes leading to the interior. All he had to do was manipulate the right knobs and levers, and he could find whatever answer he was looking for. But after several moments, the feeling of crystalline omniscience slipped away. He made a mental grab for it, trying to get it back, but it was gone, if it had ever been there at all.

He wondered if today was the day he was going to die.

* * *

Jack walked into Apothecary, a bar he liked in the busy front part of the Plaka. It was early evening. He felt good, having just done a blast of meth in the hotel room before coming out. He was still savoring the unsullied pleasure of the first hit, before it got all mixed up with sourness and neediness. The bar wasn't crowded yet, which was how he liked it. It gave him a chance to settle in.

He ordered a Dewar's on the rocks and took a seat at a small round table with a full view of the room. He had a hip flask full of cheap whiskey in his back left pocket, but he usually ordered his first drink from the house. He'd found the badly dinged-up pewter flask at the Camdentown flea market several years before; it was unusually thin, making it more comfortable to carry than most.

He only drank whiskey when he was speeding; otherwise he didn't much like the stuff. Speed gave him the pleasurable sensation of having his "on" personality, his social 'A' game, but it had jagged edges as well. His system would race, and at one point or another he'd become fidgety in the extreme. His jaw would clench, sometimes till it hurt. The image he had of being in this state came from a description he'd read of the famed Neal Cassady at an outdoor gathering of hippies, bikers, and musicians, standing off to one side by himself, one-handedly flipping and catching a hammer continuously for almost an hour straight, so much energy zooming through his wired system that he was lost in a relentless need to let off steam. For Jack, the whiskey smoothed out the edges and calmed him down a few notches so he could enjoy the feeling of power surging through him. And it had another curious effect—when the high of the drug ebbed, or even sagged outright, the hard liquor, usually energy sapping, seemed to actually give the speed a slight boost, as if igniting the dregs of the drug and giving him extra propellant to make it to the next mood upswing. The whiskey seemed to make the fuel burn more evenly, like cruise control for his roaring system. It numbed his aching tooth as well.

Mick Jagger growled from the bar's loudspeakers: "Don't want to be your slave." Jack was pretty sure it was Billy Preston sounding righteous on the organ. He sat back in his chair and sipped the amber liquid with the taste he'd never quite acquired, relaxing as best he could with his insides revving. He of course knew his sense of well-being was chemically induced—he tried hard not to allow himself delusions—but he'd take it all the same. He was in the mood for a night of hanging out, bar-hopping, maybe chasing some women—mostly for the ego-food, a drug in its own right, maybe later on for sex, though that had become less of a draw of late, for reasons he didn't fully understand, or care to try.

He looked around and to his surprise saw the tough-looking guy from the restaurant earlier that day sitting by himself on a stool where the short side of the L-shaped bar met the wall, a beer in front of him. Jack studied him again. He definitely had a formidable look—thick, fleshy nose, looked to have been broken at some point, maybe more than once, strong jaw, and the faint scars on his face. He had a little bit of a Neanderthal look, but Jack was pretty sure he sensed intelligence behind his eyes. He was wearing a blue denim button-down shirt, sleeves rolled up revealing thick hirsute forearms—a tattoo on the left one; Jack couldn't make out the image. The hair didn't seem to grow as thickly on the decorated patch of skin. Khaki trousers, shapeless and grease-stained, and weathered canvas boat shoes.

He seemed out of place. Not that you didn't get all kinds in Greece— the islands received a wide swath of humanity. But the guy had the air of a blue-collar worker—his hands looked to be in rough shape, and there was an intangible element about him suggesting a close acquaintance with serious manual labor. If he were American, you didn't often see that type of American outside the US. In parts of the Caribbean, yes, and Mexican beach towns, but that's about as far afield as they usually got.

For the second time that day, but with increased curiosity, Jack wondered what the guy's story was. The guy glanced around, and his gaze passed over Jack without pause. He still didn't seem very approachable, but Jack decided he was going to try to talk to him before the evening was out. It was the type of thing he did when he was speeding. *No hurry, though*. Jack resumed his buzzed people watching. The bar began to fill up.

For a while, he watched two tacky women tourists in their late thirties being hustled by two younger Greek guys. It always struck him as weird when people so obviously looked their parts, as if they'd been sent over from Central Casting. Both women were marginally attractive, overly thin—one was downright bony looking. They'd made various inexpert attempts to glamorize themselves—the skeletal woman had bleached blonde hair, and both wore enough makeup to project from a stage to the back row, plus brightly colored vacation clothes and lots of jewelry, gold in color though unlikely in substance. Insecurity shimmered in the air around them. The guys weren't any better. Their thing was they were extremely fit; they obviously worked out. They wore shiny shirts unbuttoned almost to their navels, hard as it was to believe that anyone still embraced such a cheesy look, and too tight trousers. They were making a big effort to entertain the ladies, talking animatedly and smiling like crazy. The women seemed flattered, though not entirely comfortable. Jack wondered if the women realized how transparent the situation was—a couple of female tourists approaching middle age being hustled by two gigolo types who probably made a lifestyle of picking up women like them and thought other guys envied them.

Jack considered going to the *banyo* for a boost but decided to hold off. You had to pace yourself if you wanted to get the most out of the ride. He had one of his disconnected flashes of taking careful aim with a pistol and blasting away. The imaginary act had been flickering in his brain with increasing frequency of late. He hadn't bothered to try to figure out why, beyond the obvious element of anger.

His attention was seized by the loud voices of two American guys in their mid-twenties standing nearby virtually shouting their side of a conversation with a young couple, man and woman, sitting on stools facing out from the bar toward the shouters. The Americans were jock types, muscular, and struck Jack as being from the 'burbs somewhere. They were being very friendly and boisterous with the couple. The woman sounded English, and the man spoke English with a Scandinavian accent. There was a hint of malice in the Americans' gregariousness, as if it were all an act and they didn't care if their semi-captive audience caught on.

"Hey," one of the Americans bellowed, "me and my pal here, Rick, we went on a cruise to nowhere once. You heard of 'em, right? That's exactly what they are—a cruise to nowhere. You get on a big cruise ship with a bunch of other party animals and go out to sea for a few days. And you don't go anywhere. You just go out there and party your brains out and come back. It's a cruise to nowhere—get it?"

He laughed raucously, putting his face too close to the woman's, and slapping the Scandinavian too hard on the shoulder.

"The ship is enormous," he went on in a thick, Jersey-sounding accent. "Packed with food and booze. And there's discos and gambling. It's great. We go crazy for three days straight, hardly sleep at all. That's just the kind of guys we are." He gave a big, toothy grin.

The guy named Rick exclaimed, "Hey, we wanna buy you nice people a drink. What'll you have?"

The couple declined, but Rick ordered four tequila shots anyway and insisted that they all down them together. The couple didn't seem well established; they may well have just met on vacation. The Americans were openly coming on to the woman, but not excluding the Scandinavian. In fact, they were being extra friendly to him, as if it were all a big joke. For his part, the Scandinavian, blond and frail, was beginning to show signs of strain. He tried to assert his position with the woman a bit, while at the same time trying to project going along with the Yanks' fake bonhomie. As for the woman, she seemed mildly inebriated and not completely tuned into the situation, maybe viewing it as merely a typical holiday encounter—interacting with people from different walks of life and all that.

Jack knew the kind of guys the Americans were. In his own way, he was a pretty big asshole himself, but he wasn't the kind of asshole these guys were. They were doing it for kicks and giggles. Being jerks and seeing where it led.

A skinny black man with dreads walked by the foursome, carefully carrying several beers, and the "cruise to nowhere" guy brayed at him, "Yo, bro. How you doing? Got any ganja?"

The black man glanced over his shoulder with a puzzled look and continued across the room. The American called after him, "Hey, get yourself a drink on us." He turned back to the couple and said, "Hey, those guys are only good at basketball. Know what I mean?"

Rick came out with a loud guffaw. Discomfort showed on the couple's faces, along with a strained friendliness. The shouters probably noticed this as readily as Jack, and took it as a signal they were getting somewhere and it was time to take the fun and games to the next level.

Jack noticed that the tough-looking guy at the end of the bar was taking all this in too.

Soon, the assholes began dropping the friendly guise and their nastiness rose to the surface. Their laughter became increasingly harsh. The girl belatedly woke up to the negative vibe and shifted on her stool to link herself more with the Scandinavian. If they'd been a more established couple, they probably would have extracted themselves, but as it was, they were off balance.

Rick leaned forward and poked the Scandinavian in the chest with his finger, saying, "Hey, man, that's a nice shirt. Where'dja get it?"

The Scandinavian tilted back away from the finger but didn't otherwise respond.

"Imagine how good it would look on me," Rick said with a big grin. His friend laughed so loudly it was ridiculous. People looked over.

Jack pointed his right hand like a pistol—forefinger sticking out, thumb up—at the back of the "cruise to nowhere" guy, and slowly pulled the imaginary trigger, making a muffled shooting sound. Shifted his aim to Rick's back and mock-shot him as well. He saw the intimidating guy watching him.

A speed-induced impulse came over Jack. He knew right away it was an idiotic idea, but such brainstorms were an integral part of who he was, and, depending on his mood, he gave himself a large amount of leeway in terms of acting on them. Not giving himself a chance to think it over, he forced himself to stand up and walk over to the guy at the end of the bar.

"'Scuse me. I saw you watching those two scumbags over there and was wondering if maybe you'd like to, uh, maybe go over there with me and . . . intervene?"

The guy gave Jack a look like, *What the hell are you going on about?*

Jack stared back in a sort of daze brought on by the extreme weirdness of what he was doing, plus the mix in his system of synthetic chemicals with just-triggered organic ones. The guy looked Jack up and down—he was thin, six feet tall, messy long hair, overall a bit unkempt, far from formidable looking. The guy looked Jack in the eyes and seemed to conclude something. Shook his head and said, "Nope, not me."

Jack was left standing there with his proverbial dick hanging out. The room around him seemed to recede instantly, and a sensation came over him of being enclosed in a body-sized bubble. The bar and the people all around him became blurred, the sounds muffled. There was a hammer-like pounding in his head.

He had landed himself in a sticky wicket, as the English liked to say. He could just turn around and go back to his chair. He didn't particularly care what the tough guy thought. But the mix of things that had goaded him in the first place still churned inside. And he'd long held the belief that physical fights were something a guy should get into every so often, in situations that called for them. He believed that most guys' fear of fighting came from not knowing it wasn't that bad to get hurt. Once you accepted you would probably get injured and it was something you could live with, your fear became something you could quash, and you could wade in that much more easily. When he was younger, he'd forced himself to get into a few altercations where he was clearly outmatched so he could learn this twisted lesson.

As he stood there and accepted what he was about to do, more jolts of adrenaline and fear shot through him, combining with the methamphetamine, the ingredient that made him feel like he was actually able to do things.

He was going to get his ass kicked, maybe badly. Hopefully it wouldn't mean an emergency room, which would be a serious drag. It wouldn't be the first time.

As far back as he could remember, part of him had felt like he deserved to get hurt every so often. In the past, driven by strong compulsions, he'd done things solely to risk doing himself damage—once turning a car going about twenty into a large tree; another time jumping from the roof of a three-story house into a big pile of snow, actions which, if he were lucky, he could emerge from unscathed, but could also very well result in serious injury. Fate had smiled on him on both occasions. Once, he eliminated the element of chance and smashed his forehead against a wall without holding back, again and again, until it bled.

These thoughts flashed through his head in a matter of moments. He was still standing in front of the guy he'd insanely thought was going to help him. He knew there was only one way to go forward, just like when he'd first stood up from his chair—push the override button and go. He knew it could be done—by just doing it. It was that simple. He wrenched himself around and walked toward the assholes.

As he covered the short distance, he willed himself to shut down, become like an automaton. With a distinctly nauseous feeling, he digested what was about to happen to him.

He tapped the "cruise to nowhere" guy on the shoulder and said, without being able to get much tone into his voice, "'Scuse me. Me and my friend over there"—he nodded over his shoulder toward the end of the bar, and the assholes looked—"we thought maybe you fellas would like to lay off these nice people." Jack glanced at Rick, then back at the cruise guy. Everything was roaring around him. His imagined bubble now contained both him and the assholes. Everything else was hazy, indistinct.

The Americans looked at him blankly for a moment. They seemed medium drunk. The cruise guy glanced over Jack's shoulder again at his "friend," then looked back at Jack, a big grin spreading over his face.

"You know," he said in a mock-gracious way, "I think you might be right. Yeah." He nodded. "Rick, come on, let's go have a few beers with this dude. But I'm getting tired of this place. Let's try a new spot, know what I mean? Leave these love-birds to themselves." Turning to the couple—they could barely take in what was going on—he said, "Hey, it's been great hanging with you folks. You're loads of fun. But we're gonna go have a few brewskis with our new buddy here. Catch you later."

Turning back to Jack, he said, "After you," with an exaggerated flourish.

Raw terror flooded Jack, despite his efforts to clamp down on it and maintain self-control. He knew his best move would be to force things right there in the bar, where there would be a limit as to how far things could go. But as if his will had been drained from him, he followed the guy's direction and walked stiffly toward the door. The assholes trailed behind.

Outside, without looking back, Jack turned right and then around a corner into a narrow street. The Americans were about a dozen feet back, seemingly in no hurry. Jack was so chock-full of dread he could barely walk steadily. There were a few boutiques on the street and some people strolling, so he kept walking. A small alley came up on his left and he turned into it. It was empty, and he turned and backpedaled several steps. He began to hyperventilate with a raspy sound. Felt hysteria coming on and thought he might start shrieking uncontrollably, like an insane person. The assholes stopped about ten feet away, staring at him. They seemed momentarily uncertain, as if it occurred to them they might be dealing with a nut job, and whatever that might mean.

They split apart and came toward him. Jack crouched. As they closed in, Jack faked toward the cruise guy on his right. Rick moved in from the left, and Jack turned fast and swung at him, focusing intently on the side of his jaw. He knew from past bad experiences that most punches miss, and he desperately wanted this one to connect. He didn't squarely catch Rick's jaw, but hit him solidly in front of his ear. Rick's head snapped sideways and he stumbled.

That was the last punch Jack landed. The cruise guy tackled him, and Rick recovered quickly and joined in with a flurry of vicious blows. Jack managed to scramble to his feet once, swinging wildly, hoping to connect. But a tremendous shot struck his temple, and that was the end of his efforts. The assholes beat the shit out of him, pounding him repeatedly without restraint.

He managed to get facedown and cover up as best he could, oblivious to everything, even the grit of the alley sticking to his bloody face. A tooth seemed to be missing from his mouth. Rick finished with a full leg-swing kick to the ribs. Fortunately he was wearing sneakers.

CHAPTER 3

Jenkins handed the powerful binoculars to Jack, who focused them on the bright white villa. By the pool, he saw two black men sitting in straight-back chairs and a white woman getting up from a lounge chair. She wore only a purple bikini bottom, held together at the hips by gold rings. She was statuesque, and, with the magnification, it was clear her ample breasts were defying gravity more than nature intended. The black men were dressed in street clothes, and one of them had a rifle on his lap. Jack was momentarily shocked by the sight of the weapon, a reaction that made no sense. The men watched as the virtually naked woman sauntered toward the villa in towering platform sandals.

* * *

Jenkins sat on his barstool and took a swig of Carlsberg, wondering what the hell that was about. He'd recognized the scrawny weird guy from the restaurant earlier. He'd known then that the guy wanted to talk to him. Jenkins had a sixth sense sometimes. It had always been like that, even when he was young. Like the time in one of the various foster homes that had basically been dormitories for him. He'd been sitting at the kitchen table one evening and somehow knew the foster father was going to take the iron skillet from the top of the stove and smash it into the side of the head of the wise-cracking, slow-on-the-uptake foster kid sitting next to him. And within a minute, it happened. Jenkins had stood up, gone into another room, returned with a baseball bat, and slammed it into a comparable spot on the father's head, with what turned out to be near-lethal consequences, as well as his first stint in reform school.

He hadn't felt like talking to the scrawny guy earlier, so he'd eaten his food quickly and left while the guy was in the john.

When Jenkins saw him sitting at the table in the bar, he knew he was gonna come over and talk to him. But Jenkins was comfortable on his barstool by the wall and didn't feel like moving, so he resigned himself to it this time. He was good at driving people away when necessary.

But when the guy did come over, Jenkins wasn't prepared for what he had to say—something about helping him deal with some jerks down the bar. The guy was high on something for sure. His pupils were enormous, filling almost all the green of his eyes.

If there were a creed Jenkins would have claimed to believe in, it was "look out for yourself," along with the corollary, "don't look out for anybody else." 'Cause no one else is gonna look out for you, and if it ain't your problem, it ain't your problem. He'd learned these lessons in too many hard ways to count growing up on the mean streets of Pittsburgh. And these beliefs had been reinforced emphatically during two stints at juvenile detention, which had proven even more dangerous than the streets.

He had a contrary impulse in him, though, a visceral abhorrence for bullies. Always had. It came from somewhere deep inside, and had savage results when combined with his skills at inflicting mayhem, which he was okay with. He'd been paid for his skills at times, and knew how to empty himself of self-control and human restraint. He wasn't proud of this, but wasn't ashamed either. He even knew how to fight to the death, not an easy thing to find inside yourself.

So there had been times when he'd broken his self-imposed rule about not looking out for other people. And when he did, something brutal and primitive came out in him.

He had to admit the two guys hassling the couple were assholes. Now they were outside with the messed-up do-gooder, who hadn't struck him as having a helpful bone in his body. So what the fuck was he doing? He was gonna get hurt. That much was sure. Unless he had some none-too-obvious skills for sudden balls-out violence. And even then . . .

Jenkins drained the rest of his beer and ordered another. He thought about the boat he'd been supposed to pick up in Piraeus a few days earlier and drive solo to a destination he was gonna be given. The boat would almost definitely contain a large cache of weapons and ammunition, though he hadn't been told that and wouldn't ask. *Where the hell are the Brits and the goddamn boat?* he thought. *What's the goddamn holdup?*

He sank into himself where he was usually able to find a certain blankness he was comfortable with. Despite the social nature of bars, it never occurred to him to strike up a conversation with a stranger. And notwithstanding the scrawny guy, people didn't often try to talk to him.

The two Americans re-entered the bar noisily, in blatant good spirits. One of them declared loudly to the other, "We destroyed that punk. Let's do some more shots." "Wooly Bully" was blaring over the sound system. After seeing who it was, Jenkins turned to face the bar. He had a bad feeling. The jerks were revved up. They moved through the crowd, one of them announcing loudly, "I like this place." They moved into a gap at the bar next to Jenkins, and called over to the European couple, "Hey, folks, how you doin'?"

They ordered tequila shots, and Jenkins sensed something coming. The drinks arrived, and the American who did most of the talking turned to him and said boisterously, "Hey, buddy, how you doin'? Lemme buy you a drink. What'll you have?"

Jenkins spun on his stool, simultaneously coming to his feet, and planted his fist deep in the guy's gut. And in an almost continuous movement, grabbed the back of his head and smashed his face down onto the bar, breaking a full shot glass with his mouth. Glass and booze and blood splattered. Jenkins turned toward the other guy, Rick. The first guy slumped to the floor, the fight completely gone out of him. The area around them had cleared instantly. The bartender was yelling something in Greek. Rick stepped toward Jenkins and swung wildly. Jenkins leaned back, let the punch go by, then quickly stepped forward, throwing a straight left that caught Rick squarely in the eye, snapping him upright. He followed with a roundhouse right that smashed into Rick's jaw with a sickening crunch. Rick went down like somebody had flipped his off switch. He tried to rise but couldn't manage to get to all fours. The first guy was moaning on the floor, holding his maimed face. Jenkins looked around, turned, and walked toward the door.

Standing in the doorway, holding his side, his face a bashed-up bloody mess, was Jack. Jenkins stopped and looked at him. "C'mon, we should get out of here," he said.

Jenkins quickly led them through the tangle of streets. He wanted to put some distance between them and the bar, especially with Jack's beat-up face, a glaring connection to the brawl. Jack managed to keep up for about five minutes, holding his side, then called out from about twenty feet behind, "Hey, man, slow down. We're okay."

Jenkins stopped and looked back in the direction they came from. Jack was deeply grateful for the pause. The left side of his ribcage throbbed every time he took a deep breath.

"Let's get off the street," said Jenkins. "Do you know another bar?"

"Yeah, I know a place." Jack looked around, getting his bearings. "It's not far from here, I think."

He led the way. The speed in his system had worn off and he craved more. His body began to feel as if it were loaded down with lead weights. But he wasn't in a bad mood. In fact, he could feel a glimmer of good spirits. Something had happened. Something that made him feel sharply alive. And this stranger was something. Jack wasn't sure what. But it was enough to perk up his flat-lined interest in life. Besides, he had more speed with him and would be able to do it soon enough.

He realized the missing tooth was the problem one, which maybe solved that problem. *Stroke of good luck*, he thought. The gap in his teeth wouldn't be noticeable unless he smiled widely.

As they walked, Jenkins said, "Man, you are one fucked-up guy. What the hell was that all about?"

"Eh, I don't know." Jack shrugged, limping along. "I've been . . . I've been in a bad head lately. And those guys were such total assholes."

"Yeah, but why'd you come up to me? Ask me to join your crazy plan?"

"I don't know. I saw you watching 'em, thought maybe they were pissing you off too. And you looked like you knew how to handle yourself. For some reason, I thought you'd say yes. And we'd . . ." He trailed off. "Christ, I wasn't wrong about you. What happened back in the bar? What set you off?"

"They tried to buy me a drink." That seemed to be the whole answer. Then he added, "As long as they weren't fucking with me, it wasn't my problem. But when they started up their bullshit up with me, I wasn't gonna wait . . . Guys like that, they're not the real thing. It's good for 'em to see what the real world is like once in a while."

Jack considered the different levels of violence in the world, from a slap in the face to trapping somebody in a burning tire, and how one level can unexpectedly encounter a whole other level and get eviscerated. This guy obviously had a talent for savagery that went well beyond the norm. Jack wondered how stable he was. "You were ferocious. Where'd you learn to do that?"

The guy didn't respond as they arrived at Timmy's bar and went in.

What Jenkins didn't say, didn't acknowledge even to himself, was that it hadn't been entirely clear the assholes were gonna start up their bullshit with him, but Jenkins hadn't been about to wait and see.

It was noisy and crowded inside. Jack headed straight to the bathroom where he cleaned up his face as best he could and did a couple of healthy snorts. A strong, pleasurable swell of artificial well-being swept through him, and his sliver of a good mood filled out nicely. His aches and pains receded.

When he came out, the guy already had a beer, and Jack got one too.

"By the way, I'm Jack Ferris," he said, extending his hand.

"Jenkins. Roy Jenkins."

They found a place to stand along one of the walls, and within a few minutes some people left and Jack was able to grab a stool so he could rest his battered body.

There were a lot of locals there that night, and the foreigners were backpacking types. People stared at Jack's mauled face. Timmy was busy, her curly blonde mane moving through the crowd. She was dressed in faded jeans, Converse high-tops, and a white T. Definitely a plus for the bar.

After awhile, she came over and said, "Jesus! What happened to you?"

"Eh, I did something stupid and got my ass kicked." Jack grinned crookedly. "But Jenkins here, he cleaned house. Big time. He was barbaric. He demolished the guys. A virtuoso display of violence."

Timmy looked at Jenkins with curiosity and frowned.

"It was just a bar fight," he said.

"Not like any bar fight I've ever seen," said Jack. "Timmy, this is . . . What did you say your first name was?"

"Roy."

"Timmy, Roy. Roy, Timmy."

They nodded at one another.

"You still haven't told me what happened," Timmy said to Jack.

Jack gave her a sketchy account, and when he got to end of the disaster in the alley, said, "I'm sitting there beat to shit, and I figured I'd go back in and ask Jenkins here to have a drink with me. Figured I'd at least earned that for my trouble. And as I walk back in, Jenkins goes medieval on the assholes."

Jenkins said, "Most bar fights are won by the guy who uses extreme violence first. If it doesn't work, you pay big time. Whatever mercy the other guy had flies right out the window."

Timmy gave a look of revulsion. She said testily to Jenkins, "I know why *he* did it. He's wrong in the head. But why you?"

"That's the best part," Jack answered. "They tried to buy him a drink. They tried to buy the wrong guy a drink." He laughed, making him wince and clutch his side.

Timmy looked at Jenkins, then back at Jack. She shook her head and walked away.

"Well, that's Timmy," Jack said as they watched her go.

"She ain't happy."

"Yeah, well." Jack shrugged. Shrugging was another thing Jack did well. And often. Conveying fully, he hoped, the fuck he did not give.

The two men drank and talked late into the night, though Jack did most of the talking, the drug driving him to hold forth on an array of topics. He tried a few times to draw Jenkins out, but Jenkins was evasive. He was vague and didn't usually string more than a few sentences together, making for silences in which Jack couldn't resist resuming his rants. He did learn that Jenkins was in Athens to meet some Brits for work, but they hadn't showed. And Jenkins referred to living in Tunisia recently, working construction on a massive hydroelectric dam. "I worked underground for weeks on end pouring concrete for the tunnels that'll channel water to the turbines. The dam is gonna generate enough electricity to light up half of North Africa."

He also said he was originally from Pittsburgh and had done a couple of hitches in the army. But that was about all Jack got out of him. He seemed closer to forty-five than the forty Jack had initially thought. At some point, Jack realized that while his first impression of Jenkins had been of menace, that wasn't quite right. He definitely gave off an air of being exceedingly tough in a fight, and he didn't seem easily intimidated at all, but he wasn't sinister, which made him less scary. Jack thought maybe he'd discerned a crack in Jenkins' apparent stone wall of self-assurance, but wasn't sure. He hadn't been very perceptive lately.

Jack rambled on about his travels, how he'd met Timmy. She'd been working as a crew member on a yacht out for a lengthy expedition and was getting fed up with it when she met Jack in the Seychelles, and left the boat.

At one point, Jenkins asked Jack again why he'd gotten in the fight, and Jack went on about how it made him feel alive. After a few minutes of his blather, Jenkins said, "You mean you did it 'cause you were bored?"

Jack shrugged and nodded.

As the night wore on, Jack made more visits to the bathroom. On his return one time, Jenkins said, "You're gonna get really fucked up with all the booze and whatever it is you're doing in there."

"That's right."

Around two in the morning, Jack started babbling about how he'd lost his love of travel and had come back to Greece because it was his old standby. It was the first foreign country he'd ever visited, and it had scored a bull's-eye back then. Ever since, he'd found it rejuvenated his spirits when he felt the need. He indicated now was one of those times, and the matter had acquired some urgency.

"The islands are fantastic," he said. "There's over a thousand of them, and you can find whatever you're looking for. Party islands, remote isolation, amazing natural beauty, especially after your eyes get used to the rocky islands with hardly any greenery—the rocks have an extraordinary beauty all of their own. And people come to the islands from all over the world. You can be on a beach in Mykonos with people from twenty-five different countries. It's an incredible coming together, and everyone's in a social mood. You should check out a few before you leave."

"You going to any of them soon?"

"Yeah, in the next day or so. Want to come along?"

"Three's a crowd."

"Yeah, well, I'm not sure Timmy will be coming."

"Why not?"

"We seem to have reached the end of the line."

Jenkins didn't say anything.

"I'm an asshole," Jack said. "And don't for a moment think I'm any less of one for admitting it."

CHAPTER 4

Jack was woken by Jenkins jostling his shoulder. They were on the private island. The motorboat was tied to a tree branch hanging low over the cove, its prow pointed out toward the sea. He couldn't believe he'd fallen asleep. It didn't seem possible under the circumstances. But the bed of pine needles covering the ground had been so inviting. So comfortable when he stretched out on it. Something inside him must have powerfully needed to shut down.

"He's there," Jenkins said quietly. "I saw him swimming. He's a big bastard."

* * *

"The thing is," said Jack, "what with terrorism and all these days, it's getting harder and harder to carry drugs on planes."

He and Jenkins were sitting on the open top deck of the early morning ferry from the mainland town of Pelios to Kyros, an island in the Sporades group. There was no airport on Kyros, which Jack said was what kept it being one of the gems of the Greek isles. There was no one else on the open deck. It was sunny but there was a brisk wind, and all the other passengers were on enclosed lower decks, including Timmy, who'd gotten coffee and was reading a used Kurt Vonnegut novel she'd been excited to find in an Athens bookshop, in English.

Jack and Jenkins sat on deck chairs made of wood and weather-bleached gray canvas; the original color was anybody's guess. They'd turned their chairs to look over the left side of the boat where a series of small uninhabited islands gave the illusion of floating by. The wind whipped around them and felt good, invigorating. Seagulls glided effortlessly on the air currents behind the ferry without even a hint of wing movement, and beyond them receding in the distance were the towering craggy mountains of the mainland.

The sky was a deep azure, cloudless, and the air was exceptionally clear, without even a trace of haze. The horizon was a crisp line, and the detailed patterns of the rocks on the passing islands were in sharp focus. The simple act of seeing was fresh and pleasing. Jack almost felt good to be alive, though the skin below his eyes was still deep purple from his foolhardy fisticuffs. At least his toothache was gone.

When he'd first read *Zorba the Greek*, he'd come across the passage: "Happy is the person who is deemed worthy, before he dies, to sail the Aegean." As he read the words, they struck him right away as containing a profound truth, though he had no basis for thinking that beyond intuiting that Kazantzakis was a wise and perceptive writer. He decided to find out for himself as soon as he could, and by the time he was eighteen, an orphaned loner, he'd gone out on a small sailboat, solo, on the legendary sea, and discovered that Kazantzakis had indeed written the truth. Skimming across the sea of so many myths, with its innumerable shades of impossible blue, powered only by the wind, Jack had felt something akin to happiness.

"It used to be," he went on, "you could carry drugs through just about any airport in the world. As long as you didn't act stupid and weren't coming in from Bogota or someplace like that, you didn't run into any problems. There was only customs to worry about back then, no real security. And all customs did was glance through your bags, if that. Nobody frisked you unless you acted like an idiot. You could carry drugs on your person, right in your pocket if you wanted to push your luck.

"Now, with terrorism, they do random body searches and go through your carry-on stuff with a fine-toothed comb. You can put drugs in the bags you check through, and when you arrive switch 'em to your person to go through customs, but the switch is risky. You never know who's watching in baggage claim. One-way mirrors, people standing around. So, now you've got to get more elaborate. And all because of terrorism. It's outrageous—goddamn terrorists making it a hassle for recreational drug users like me," he concluded with mock indignation.

"Recreation?" said Jenkins. "Is that what you call it?"

"Yeah, well."

"Same thing with guns," said Jenkins. "Used to be you could carry guns on planes. Easy. People did it all the time. Not anymore. Though I heard they're coming up with a new handgun made of some kind of plastic. Won't show up on metal detectors."

"You used to carry guns on planes?" Jack looked at him with surprise.

"No, not me."

"So, how do you know about it?"

"Doesn't take a genius to figure it out. One day there weren't any metal detectors. Next day they were everywhere."

There's more to the story, thought Jack, but he waited to see if Jenkins would say more.

Incongruous screeches came from the gulls floating gracefully on the wind currents created by the ship.

"I've known people who did," Jenkins went on.

Jack considered this. "What were they doing carrying guns on planes?"

"Forget it," said Jenkins, shaking his head.

"Aw, come on . . ."

"No, drop it."

Jack started to press but decided to leave it for the moment. He stood up and stretched, forgetting his tender left ribs and arching his back harshly. Wincing in pain, he gingerly sat back down. The ferry passed close to an island, and he studied the intricate skein of cracks in a massive rock face.

"Actually," he said in a flippant tone, "I can sort of relate to being a terrorist." He paused for a reaction from Jenkins, but Jenkins just massaged the eagle tattoo on his forearm. "I mean, most people to some extent can understand terrorists who do it because someone did some horrible shit to them, like killed their kid with a missile or something like that. But pure terrorists, the kind they've got in Germany and Italy, the Baader-Meinhof Gang, the Red Brigades, they're a lot harder to understand. They say they're doing it in the name of anarchy or to spread chaos, wreak havoc on the system. Most people hear about terrorists like that, and they're completely baffled. They think, *I don't get it.*

Why do they do it? What makes them tick? They're living in developed countries with a decent standard of living. Why would they want to attack their own society? Blow up buildings, kill civilians? Why would people who could pretty easily have an okay life want to do stuff like that, especially if they're educated? But I can sort of halfway understand those terrorists."

Jack liked to think he was well informed about world affairs, but his knowledge was often superficial and faulty.

"You are so full of shit," said Jenkins.

"Yeah, well."

Jenkins yawned and scratched his stomach. "Okay, go on. Tell me how you can relate to being a terrorist."

"Well, the terrorists I'm talking about, the pure terrorists in Europe, I figure they're really doing it 'cause they're bored and angry. And for the excitement, the jolt. Plus it makes them feel important. They say they've got a cause, but do they really? I mean, what the hell is anarchy anyway? Chaos? How can that be a good thing for almost anybody? The European terrorists are full of shit. They're just bored, angry people working out their issues and looking for kicks. And me, well, I'm plenty bored and angry, and I've got a ton of issues. And I'm always looking for excitement.

"The way I'm different is that, for some baffling reason, I need to get my thrills from doing the right thing. And for something that matters. I don't know why. I'm pretty much without morals. But for some reason I need my excitement to be achieved by something with morality on its side. The excitement wouldn't be satisfying if I got it by doing some bad shit. It's too easy to get your kicks from doing bad stuff. Like cheating to win at a game. The pure terrorists, though, they don't make any such distinctions, and, like I said, a big part of why they do their evil stuff is just plain boredom and getting excitement, though they'd never admit it. They maintain their terrorism is motivated by some higher purpose, some intellectually concocted drivel."

Jenkins stared steadily at the horizon, no reaction.

"I read this book once," Jack went on. "It was a true story about these two young guys in their mid-twenties, living somewhere in southern California, I think. They were friends from when they were kids, altar boys together, but they'd drifted apart. Anyway, one of them got a job through his dad at a major defense contractor, which required some level of government clearance because of access to classified information. The other guy turned out to be pretty much of a sleazebag—a small-time drug dealer, always on the hustle for a quick buck. They still saw each other once in a while, and somehow they came up with this idea. The guy who worked for the defense contractor would sneak classified documents out of his work, and they'd sell them to the Russians. It sounds ludicrous, but it really happened.

"The defense contractor kid later claimed he was motivated by some vague anti-government sentiments, and the sleazy guy was definitely motivated partly by the money, but it was obvious to me from reading the book that the main reason they did it was 'cause they were bored and wanted some excitement in their lives." Jack scratched a five-inch scar on his right knee, a remnant from the brief time in boarding school when he'd tried to fit in and played soccer.

"So, they went ahead and did it. The sleazy guy went down to Mexico City to the Russian Embassy there to make the arrangements. He had a lot of trouble convincing the Russians he was for real, but eventually he got them to come around. And for a short time, these two guys actually sold classified US documents to the Russians. They were real-life spies. They got caught pretty quickly because they were bungling amateurs. And they got sent to prison for long stretches." Jack looked at Jenkins to see if he was still listening—it wasn't clear, but Jack assumed he was.

"When I read the book, I felt like I understood them. They did it for the kicks. They were bored. Plain and simple."

"And they wound up in jail," said Jenkins.

"Yeah, because they were stupid. And their adventure wasn't even all that interesting. But still, the point is I can understand why they did it."

Jack lapsed into silence.

Eventually Jenkins said, "So, what are you gonna do, Jack? What are you gonna do to get some excitement into your life? Other than getting your ass kicked in bar fights."

"Damned if I know." Jack grinned. "But I have had an idea. Benevolent terrorism. Right now, the governments of developed countries fight terrorism with their hands tied behind their backs. They're not allowed to do all kinds of things that would definitely get results. And I'm not just talking about breaking a few laws, which I'm sure the US and other governments already do. I'm talking about behaving just like the terrorists, doing the same horrible shit to them that they do to innocent people. Turn the tables on them, make them live in terror. See how much they like it.

"My idea is that the government of one of the developed countries creates a secret organization, hidden to the point of invisibility, completely unacknowledged—maybe based in an anonymous office building in a large foreign city—and appoints a few extremely capable people with the right skill sets and experience to run it. The government gives them a bucket load of funding up front, deposited in a numbered foreign bank account, available for them to draw on. Enough so they have all the money they need to set up the organization and operate it for at least two years without coming back to the government for more. From then on, the government has as close to zero contact with them as possible.

"The guys in charge would carefully recruit people with the right kind of psychological makeup and background to function in top secret and do horrific things to bad people, but balanced and grounded enough so they don't go off the deep end. And they arrange for the recruits to be trained to the max with skills in killing, covert operations, and dishing out terror. They arrange state-of-the-art backup support, technicians with the best surveillance equipment, and top analysts, still being very careful to choose the right kind of people to be okay with the work and keep it completely secret.

"There'd be no acknowledgment that the organization even exists, no verifiable connection to any government. The absolute minimum number of people in the host government would even know about it. There'd be no written references to it, except as absolutely necessary, and even then only by way of a code name without specifics.

"Then, the operatives would be turned loose on the terrorists of the world, no holds barred, no legal restraints. They'd do whatever it takes.

Fight terror with terror. See how long the terrorists stick with their evil ways when there's some invisible group out there turning their lives into a living hell, and the lives of everyone they're close to. All concepts of civilized behavior would be thrown out the window. The terrorists wouldn't even know for sure where it was coming from, making it all the more terrifying.

"The public would love it, even though they wouldn't know who was doing it. It'd be like Charles Bronson in *Death Wish* where he goes out by himself at night in New York City, armed with a handgun, deliberately looking to get mugged. And shoots the muggers. In the movie, the police figure out there's a vigilante shooting would-be muggers, but they don't know who he is. The newspapers make it a front-page story, and the public eats it up. Journalists poll people on the street for their reactions, and almost to a person, they applaud the vigilante. The average New Yorker was sick and tired of being afraid on their own streets, in their own neighborhoods, and they were over the moon that someone was doing something about it, something that had real impact. Muggings in New York dropped dramatically."

Jenkins looked at Jack for a while, as if trying to figure him out. "You got one hell of an imagination," he said eventually. "I don't know if your secret operation could be pulled off or not. But I'll tell you one thing, people like that don't exist—people who can do balls-out violence to strangers they're told deserve it, but not go off the deep end. In my experience, people who do evil shit are usually evil in the first place, and the ones that aren't eventually become evil by doing what they're doing. You've got to be careful with people. Almost everybody has bad inside 'em somewhere, and under the right circumstances it'll come out, especially if you let 'em police themselves and decide who deserves to have hell-fire brought down on 'em. But hey, that's just my opinion."

It wasn't the first time, but Jenkins' uncharacteristically long remarks confirmed to Jack again that he'd been right about there being smarts behind the crude-looking face. "You've got a point," he acknowledged. "My concept may need some fine-tuning, but I still think it's a great idea. I think it's got the potential to work wonders.

"I heard of a situation in Lebanon once, where Muslim terrorists kidnapped a high-level Russian diplomat. And within twenty-four hours, the Russians had kidnapped dozens of the terrorists' family members. Completely illegal, a war crime in fact. The Russian was promptly released unharmed. And there you have it—benevolent terrorism at work to perfection.

"And the organization wouldn't just take on terrorists. They'd take out other major bad guys around the world too. Evil dictators like Baby Doc, and that maniac in Cambodia who killed a million people trying to re-create a peasant society. Unbelievable—the guy has an idea about the way people should live, and kills over a million people to try to make it so. If he's still around, he'll be at the top of my organization's list.

"The operatives should maybe be called vigilantes, but benevolent terrorism has such a great ring to it, don't you think?"

"You know, Jack, if you ever get some real excitement in your life—the kind you're looking for—you'll get eaten alive." He laughed and pointed to a large bird in the sky, which he'd just watched swoop down onto a passing island, and was flying away with a snake squirming in its talons.

As the ferry approached Kyros Town, the only town on the island, it appeared as a haphazard cluster of whitewashed cubist structures, roughhewn like adobe dwellings, built along the curve of an enchanting little bay and up the sides of the surrounding hills. To Jack, the town was suggestive of organic modern art, if that wasn't a contradiction in terms, and at the same time exuded the phantoms and echoes from all the centuries it had quietly existed in this remote place. The ubiquitous white was dotted with vividly colored doors and shutters, mostly bright blue, a few bold green, the openings of one structure a daring purple. Roughly in the middle of town, halfway up a hillside, was a prominent sky-blue dome with a large white cross sticking up from the top. Lining the waterfront was a row of cafés and tavernas, with outdoor seating and awnings of various colors, striped and solid.

When the trio disembarked, Jack realized he'd left his jean jacket onboard and went back to get it, leaving Jenkins and Timmy standing together on the town dock.

"So, what are you doing hanging out with Jack?" she asked, not in an unfriendly way.

He looked around at his new surroundings. "I was s'posed to meet some people in Athens for a job and they didn't show. So, I figured I'd take in some of the famous Greek islands. If I'm in the way, just let me know."

"No, he's all yours," she said.

The question is, thought Jenkins, *what are you doing hanging out with a guy as messed up as Jack?*

As the motley threesome walked through the town carrying their bags, it was obvious the crooked, narrow streets had emerged without the slightest planning, and the result was truly labyrinthine. There were stairs between buildings that led unexpectedly from one level of town to another, some verging on ladder-like steep, others sloping gradually with steps several feet apart. The paving of the streets created its own unique visual—irregularly shaped, light gray flagstones, worn smooth by time and use, each outlined with thick white mortar, creating a haphazard mosaic as the village floor. Along with numerous tavernas and bars, the streets were lined with boutiques selling jewelry, ceramics, and peasant-chic clothing, plus a few art galleries here and there, mostly featuring modern art with primitive influences. One shop sold highly realistic faux antiquities. The town was extremely clean and well maintained, yet felt very much lived in. There was a strong sense of social fabric, which Jenkins liked the feel of. What he was picking up on, though he couldn't have put it into words, were the dynamics and internecine relations of a small town of longtime inhabitants going back generations.

On their first evening, the three of them went out for dinner at a taverna tucked away in a tiny plaza created by five streets and alleys coming together, where all the other patrons were obvious locals. Jack was speeding away and barely ate anything, drinking lots of the piney-tasting retsina. He discoursed at length on random topics, which was just as well since Jenkins and Timmy weren't being very talkative. At one point, he rambled on about a phase when he'd been fascinated by secret societies. "I was completely intrigued with the notion there were these associations unknown to the general public that had substantial influence over their societies. I wanted someone to walk up to me on a street one day and whisper 'Abraxas' in my ear." He laughed at the silliness of his younger self. He held forth on Rosicrucians, the Illuminati, Gnostics, and people like Nostradamus, Aleister Crowley, and Gurdjieff. Then he got onto the subject of cults and went on a diatribe about Jonestown and the people who literally drank the Kool-Aid. The power of Jim Jones' charisma confounded him, but impressed him as well. He concluded with, "Somebody said religion was invented when the first scam artist met the first fool, and I tend to think it's true. People who are seriously into religion got nothing else going on in their lives."

At one point, he said to Jenkins, "So, tell us. What was Viet Nam like?"

Jenkins had made the mistake earlier of mentioning to Jack he'd been posted there when he was in the army. He'd made clear he hadn't been in combat. After an abruptly shortened stint as a radio operator at Khe Sanh, he'd been transferred to a supply depot in the south, just outside a backwater town on the Mekong Delta called Ton Loc.

Before Jenkins could answer, Jack went on with a grin, "I mean, a warehouse gig like you had must have provided some prime opportunities to make money on the side, what with all the material passing through."

"Not really." Jenkins ruffled his mustache with scarred fingers. The truth was, though, Jack had scored a bull's-eye. After rejecting a number of approaches, Jenkins had been contacted by a guy he trusted who vouched for a group of contractors—soldiers, ex-military—looking to buy substantial amounts of ordnance. Jenkins had agreed and implemented the arrangement with strict carefulness. Over the next several months, he surreptitiously channeled munitions to the buyers in exchange for envelopes full of cash. It was easy. The army was extremely disorganized in Nam, to the point of chaos much of the time. They regularly lost track of loads of equipment, even helicopters and trucks. Some crates of rifles and ammunition, RPG launchers, were nothing.

Jenkins had never told anybody about his illegal enterprise, and Jack definitely wasn't the person he was gonna start with. Jenkins knew that when you told somebody something, no matter what assurances were made, sooner or later somebody said something to somebody. He'd acquired the difficult discipline of keeping his mouth shut, completely and permanently, about stuff that needed to stay unknown.

What Jack really wanted to hear anyway were combat stories. Jenkins had plenty of those second and third-hand, but wasn't in the mood to indulge Jack, who he could already tell was one of those guys who glorified war.

"Hey, did you ever hear about the Great Elephant Zap?" Jack asked. "Supposedly, the US military decided that elephants were helping the Viet Cong too much by carrying their supplies on jungle trails where trucks couldn't go. So, they sent out squadrons of helicopters with mounted machine guns to rain fire and brimstone down on the unlucky beasts of burden. Slaughtered entire herds. I read where even hardened gunners got disgusted."

"I never heard of that." Jenkins smiled ruefully. "But Nam was definitely a place where crazy shit like that happened all the time."

Timmy said, "I have a cousin who fought there."

"I didn't know Australians were involved in the fighting," said Jack. "I thought it was just us idiot Americans."

"Yeah, my cousin started out saying Australia had skin in the game—we weren't that far away—so we had good reason to join in. But he came back completely against the war. Said once he was there, he had to really think about what he was doing and why—killing people, risking getting himself killed. And he couldn't see the sense in it. He said it wasn't our fight. It was a war between the Vietnamese. And there was no way for us to ever get out satisfactorily, no way to win and leave."

"Yeah," said Jack, "we were fighting an enemy willing to lose a million men to our fifty thousand. And still keep going. How do you beat that?"

Later in the meal, Jack prompted Timmy to tell Jenkins about when she'd been a "rock star" back in Australia.

Jenkins looked at her with curiosity.

"I wasn't a star." She blushed. "I was just the drummer. And it was more pop than rock. It was an all-girl band called Tin Angel. We actually got signed to a record deal and put out an album. It sold decently in Australia. We weren't very good, except the lead singer. She wrote all the songs. But the rest of us, we were just in it 'cause she wanted to have an all-girl band. I didn't even know how to play the drums properly when we started. I'd played in the high school band and figured out the rest as we went along. I was lucky I had a strong natural sense of rhythm." She smiled at the memories. "It was a lot of fun—playing in clubs in front of crowds, going into the record shops and finding our album in the bins."

The dinner cost them a total of about thirteen dollars in drachmas, and they each put in.

The next morning, Jack seemed to feel some responsibility to show Jenkins around, and they took a taxi to Banana Beach at the far end of the island, riding along the picturesque southern coast, with numerous steep drops to waves crashing on rocks below. "There must be a Greek name for the beach," Jack said, but the map for tourists labeled it "Banana."

Jenkins had never understood the beach thing and was at a loss as to what to do there. Jack had brought a book called *The Magus*, which he said he was reading for the third time, and Timmy was finishing up her book from the ferry, something about a slaughterhouse. Jenkins wasn't a reader. He tried occasionally—he'd hear about some book and want to read it—but working though the sentences and extracting the meaning was a tedious baffling struggle, and he invariably gave up. To the extent he'd attended school, it had been in a purely physical sense, and not always that. He'd dropped out as soon as allowed.

Jack fell asleep in the sun while reading.

Jenkins didn't swim very well, but going in the water was of course something people did at the beach, as exemplified by the scene in front of him. So he ventured into the chilly June sea to see if there was more to the experience than he remembered. There wasn't.

Jack was burned when he woke. He draped a towel over his head and back, and sat next to Jenkins on the sand with his knees up, giving a running commentary on the women on the beach, more than half of whom were topless, including Timmy, whom he refrained from commenting on. Jenkins noticed she had lovely small breasts with nipples that seemed to permanently protrude.

Jenkins sat by himself on the small balcony of the apartment Jack had found for them in town, drinking a can of Greek beer called Mythos. Jack had bought a six-pack of it and put it in the fridge. It tasted lousy. He lit a Marlboro and enjoyed the first drag. It was early evening, a few days after they arrived.

The apartment was a one bedroom, with a main room that had a foldout couch and a kitchen area. Jack and Timmy each had a single bed in the bedroom, and Jenkins got the couch. They had their own bathroom, which Jack and Timmy were happy about; Jenkins didn't stay in hotel rooms with a shared toilet. The apartment was on the second floor in the back of a boxlike two-story building with a whitewashed stucco surface. The structure was at the back edge of town, so the balcony looked out over open land.

To Jenkins' left, about fifty yards away, a half dozen kids were playing soccer on a dirt patch. He watched the olive-skinned boys running around in the dust and late afternoon sunlight, which was virtually blinding him, but he didn't mind. At the edge of the playing area stood a donkey with its head hanging down, motionless except for the occasional flick of its tail. Beyond the scene rose the island's pine-forested hills, with the bright orange ball of the sun just above, about to start dropping behind them.

Scattered in front of Jenkins was a patchwork of vegetable gardens, a couple of rundown sheds, gnarled olive trees here and there, an abandoned car, and a discarded washing machine listing to one side. To his right were a pair of elegant village townhouses, clearly freshly painted—the usual bright white with vivid blue doors and shutters—which would have provided the balcony with a lovely view had it not been for an exceptionally thick cluster of wires strung between two tall wooden poles, crossing directly in front of the residences. Cicadas droned, though not as loudly as during the full heat of the day.

He could hear Timmy moving around inside. Jack was out somewhere. She'd already found a job at one of the harbor-front cafés, and he figured she was getting ready to go to work. Jenkins wasn't very comfortable around her, and with them alone in the apartment, he was just as glad to be out on the balcony. She hadn't been very friendly to him, not that she was being very friendly to Jack, either.

Jenkins wondered what the hell he was doing here with these two. This was not his world. Not even a little bit. The closest he'd ever come was recently in Marbella, the flashy resort town on the Costa del Sol. He'd been there at the behest of some beefy hard-drinking Englishmen, including the ones he'd been supposed to meet in Athens. The Englishmen basically lived on their motorized yachts, which they almost never took out, though they claimed to love boating. They stayed docked almost all the time in one or another of the seemingly endless, jam-packed marinas along the coast there. They were red-faced, loud, and boisterous, with leathery-looking middle-aged blond women usually hanging around, not always properly introduced. Jenkins knew the men were dangerous, or had the potential to be when the occasion arose, so he was careful around them. But they seemed to like him, tried to pull him into their rowdy, almost daily drinking parties. The truth was he hadn't been much more comfortable with them than he was with Jack and Timmy.

He still had a room in Tunis, paid up in advance for a few months yet. Some possessions. Wondered if he'd bother to go back.

He hadn't been feeling right lately. The hard-earned accord he'd achieved with the world seemed to have slipped out of place, though he couldn't put his finger on exactly how or why.

When he was sixteen, he'd been sent to juvie for the second time, basically because of the first time plus a subsequent aggravated assault, which basically meant he'd gone too far in a street fight that should have never made it onto the police radar. Once hostilities broke out, his no-holds-barred mode exploded from within, and he didn't always get it back under control as soon as he should.

There was a kid at the facility who virtually didn't talk and had a thing about being touched. He was very clear to everybody that he didn't want to ever be touched. It was obviously not a casual preference, but rather a set-in-stone fixation. For Jenkins, it was no skin off his back, and he gave the kid his space. But one of the other kids, a mean troublemaker who Jenkins had had to back down a few times himself, snuck up behind the silent kid one day and tapped him lightly on the shoulder, just a touch. That night, after lights out, the silent kid took a hot iron and pressed it against the side of the offending kid's face while he was sleeping. At the time, Jenkins wondered what it was like to be woken like that, maybe in the midst of a real dream and being yanked out of it into a real-life nightmare. He could remember the screams shooting through the darkness like lightning bolts. Howl after howl, not fading in the slightest till the kid was taken away.

Jenkins was well aware there were plenty of people with issues that went well beyond frivolous, and there were more than a few seriously damaged units out there among the population. He recognized Jack right away as a casualty, and was surprised he hadn't turned him away immediately, as he usually avoided such people. Actually, though, he realized he had turned away Jack twice, but he'd persisted and somehow broken through to Jenkins.

He thought about his time after he'd left the army in '74. Back in the States, he'd worked as "security" for a coal company in West Virginia during a long and violent miners' strike. Much later, he'd fallen into some construction work and picked up a few basic skills. Caught a big break—was in the right place at the right time to get work with Bechtel, the massive construction outfit that built the projects too gargantuan and complicated for other firms, mostly overseas, with governments picking up the tabs. They had a regular need for skilled laborers willing to work in shitty foreign countries, and Jenkins was perfect for them.

It never occurred to Jenkins to feel sorry for himself. He didn't see any reason. But he did have a vague sense there was something stunted about himself, things inside that hadn't ever had a chance to grow. And once in a while, he felt an abstract sense of want. No specifics, just want.

To his surprise, Timmy came out onto the balcony and bummed a cigarette. She stood there and smoked, looking out at the semi-rural scene. She seemed to be in a good mood, though Jenkins thought he could sense a tinge of sadness about her. He liked her standing there. He massaged his tattoo.

"Shame about the wires," she said. "The Greeks have a knack for putting them in the exact spot where they spoil the view." Jack had pointed this out to her in a number of similar cases.

To avoid seeming unfriendly, Jenkins asked, "Where did you grow up?"

"Western Sydney. A neighborhood called Punchbowl. Poor and dreary is about the only way to describe it. The highway to Melbourne is virtually in my family's back yard. My dad's a car mechanic. When he's not working, he spends most of his time at his leagues club, drinking. Big rugby fan. He likes the violence."

Jenkins had no idea what else to say. They made some small talk about her job at the café. "I'm lucky," she said. "They're not very strict about foreigners working in Greece." She finished her cigarette and left.

CHAPTER 5

Jack trudged uphill behind Jenkins, covered in a thick layer of sweat, carrying the Browning pistol in his hand. He felt nauseous. Wanted to lie down on the ground and curl up in a ball. But Jenkins just kept walking steadily uphill, like some kind of cyborg—it was unbelievable. Jack followed, feeling smothered by reluctance, the perspiration enshrouding him like a coat of lead.

He glanced over his shoulder at the sparkling blue sea and despaired that the sight didn't give him even a smidgen of the exultation it once had.

* * *

Jack watched the pretty girl in the pale salmon dress across the crowded club. He was leaning against a rough-hewn stone wall and snuck a sip of whiskey from his flask. He'd gotten a barber haircut that afternoon, out of the ordinary for him when he was on the road. His long hair was medium brown with lighter streaks from over-exposure to the sun. He'd had the barber, whose skills were limited, keep the length but try to make it look less bedraggled. He only had whiskers for a mustache and goatee, none along his jawline, though tonight he was clean shaven. He wore black jeans and a black T-shirt with a red silhouette on the front of a swirling female flamenco dancer, both freshly washed; they looked worn and hung loosely on his skinny frame.

The club was called Borzoi and had been built to resemble the inside of a cave—irregular stone walls curving upward to become an uneven ceiling—but was painted all white, so it had an underground feel without the gloom. Flashing pinpoint beams of colored light were the only illumination. Donna Summer was blaring, which Jack detested but accepted as part of the nightlife on the travel circuit—out of date but classic with broad appeal. The dance area was packed.

Beautiful shade of pink, he thought. The dress was sleeveless and made of what looked to be exceptionally soft cotton. The pale salmon went perfectly with her smooth olive skin and lustrous brown hair. She was standing with another girl, less attractive, dark haired, and they were smoking cigarettes in a practiced feminine way—elbows crooked at their sides with hands raised, holding the cigarettes at their fingertips, and every so often gracefully placing the filter tips between their glossy lips and briefly inhaling, then resuming their casual stance. The pretty girl looked very Mediterranean, young, around twenty. The dress fit the contours of her nubile figure perfectly, not too tight, not too loose. She wore flat, thin-soled sandals made of delicate strips of leather, and a simple gold necklace of tiny chain links.

She was a pretty young thing out for a summer night in the Greek islands—her time in the sun. She was a pleasure just to behold, to the extent he was capable of enjoying such small intangible things.

I'm in a strange mood, he reflected. *Having mellow thoughts and all that.* He was a bit worried about himself. He was always a bit worried about himself, but lately things seemed to have taken a turn for the weirder. He wasn't feeling as accepting of his disconnected cynical self as usual. At the beach that day, he'd read that all cynicism masked a failure to cope, and it rang true to him.

It had occurred to him awhile back that his personality was a construct. It seemed he'd built his disillusioned self out of qualities his life experience had perversely made him think were interesting and appealing. The result was almost a perfect facsimile of a normal personality, but not quite. His persona was based partly on romantic notions about being a loner, and bizarrely that depression was somehow an interesting quality. In his late teens, he'd fancied himself a Heathcliff figure. All this helped him prey on a certain type of girl and later on woman. He'd recently come to see there was nothing romantic about being the loser he was, but he still used his contrived self to fool people on occasion. He had a keen instinct for women who'd fall for it.

He gave himself a shake, trying to drive away the disquieting thoughts.

A young guy joined the two girls across the club, diminutive but very handsome with glossy hair cut stylishly—long and swooping on the sides, short in the back. He and the girl in the pale salmon dress were quite friendly to one another, standing close as they talked. They seemed to be together to Jack's disappointment, but he kept watching. There was something that made him think maybe not—the way she faced the room, the way she glowed.

She gave no sign she'd noticed him, but he assumed she had—he wasn't being subtle. The young guy drifted away and joined a group of other guys nearby. Jack tried to catch her eye, but she didn't or wouldn't look his way. A few minutes later, the guy rejoined her. It seemed maybe it was time to start looking around for other possibilities. Jack took a discreet sip from his flask and looked around the crowded room—*plenty more fish on the beach*, as he was fond of saying, though people often didn't get it and corrected him. He and Timmy had ceased having sex about three weeks back. He hadn't been functioning very well anyway, probably due to cumulative effects of the speed, or so he hoped.

The young guy wandered off again. Soon after, the girl met Jack's eyes for a moment and looked away. Before long, she looked again and held his gaze for a few moments. The next time, he smiled at her, and as she looked away she gave a little smile as well. He felt the familiar heady rush.

He continued looking her way, and the next time their eyes met, she held his gaze and they smiled openly at one another. As often happened to him when intensity swept into a situation, the part of his space in clear focus shrank instantly, leaving the rest of the area blurred, sounds muted. This time, it was as if he and the girl were enclosed in opposite ends of a large bubble with a long tubular part in between and a potent charge coursing back and forth inside. Jack loved the feeling, the sweet rush. It was one of his favorite things—the jolt of ego-juice. After several moments, she looked away. He went to the bar and ordered a Dewar's on the rocks to have something to hold in his hand, planning to go over and talk to her as soon as he got the drink.

But the goddamn guy came back. And they were quite friendly again. Maybe they *were* together. Jack wasn't inclined to approach her with the guy standing there, not unless she gave him a clear come-on look.

Jack shook his head to himself and went to the *banyo* to give his social persona a boost. As he tooted up, he had one of his unconnected flashes of shooting a powerful handgun and the kickback jerking his arm.

Recently, he'd been catching glimpses out of the corner of his left eye of what seemed like flitting shadows, but when he turned to look, there was never anything there. He thought it was a side effect of his long-term meth use; it seemed to decrease in frequency when he laid off. Nonetheless, he'd begun to think of the darting images as shadow people, somehow connected to him, not quite stalking but present, several feet away, silently watching.

When he came out of the bathroom, the guy wasn't with her, and without hesitating he walked over and said, "Hi. Do you speak English?" Unfortunately his only language, as with so many Yanks.

More unfortunately, she didn't, or almost none at all. Her girlfriend spoke a little, which helped, but he didn't want to wind up just talking to the friend. He'd dealt with language barriers before in the course of chasing women around the globe, and knew it was challenging. For it to go anywhere, the woman had to be keen and straightforward. There wasn't a lot of room for nuance or games. Being in a noisy club hindered in some ways but helped in others—everybody had trouble talking in places like that. Fortunately, as he and the girl stumbled through the preliminaries, she communicated semi-shyly with her eyes and smile, and he was pretty sure he was getting the message he wanted.

It turned out, to his surprise, she was Greek, from Athens. He didn't usually find Greek women attractive, but this one was very pretty. Nineteen years old. Her name was, of all things, Elizabeth; she tried unsuccessfully to explain how her parents had chosen it. She did manage to convey it was the last night of her holiday.

She and her girlfriend smoked Marlboro Lights constantly, as it seemed almost all young Mediterraneans did these days.

Before long, he nodded toward the dance floor, one of the best ways to hang out with someone without talking. Besides, he could tell he was going to enjoy dancing with her. He had an excess of chemically generated energy, and it wouldn't hurt to burn some off.

Dancing with her was every bit as much fun as expected—the music enveloped them, colored lasers flashed in the dark, people gyrated all around them. Jack became lost in the pulsing rhythms, his body moving without thought, propelled by the beat. He delighted in her swaying young body moving nonchalantly to the music, her smooth tan skin, lovely face, and plump lips. She seemed to be getting comfortable with him, enjoying herself. She gave him coy provocative looks—more ego-pleasure washed through him. He bathed in the excitement, the electricity of mutual raw attraction. They shimmied and pranced, moved in synch with one another. Sweated. It all made him higher. The speed roared inside him, the righteous speed. Sometimes, he thought he actually felt something like love for the insidious shit.

Eventually, they took a break. They were breathing hard, their skin and clothing moist with perspiration. He went to get drinks, but when he got back, the goddamn guy was there again. She introduced them, and he was friendly. His name was Cheseret. *Christ*, thought Jack, *what a perfect name for this guy.* He was Italian. Spoke English better than the young women, but it had a way of drying up whenever Jack tried to ask about Elizabeth, the music keeping her from hearing him make inquiries. It seemed like she and Cheseret had only met recently on holiday but were already extremely at ease with one another. Jack knew people could bond extra quickly when traveling, especially young people. He couldn't quite get a fix on the situation. She was still being friendly to him and acting interested, but the erotic sparks between them were fizzling. Because of the language barrier, he couldn't simply lean in close to her ear and ask her what the story was. She conversed easily with Cheseret in Italian.

"Elizabeth will come to Rome next week to visit me," Cheseret said to Jack. "You should come too."

Jack gave a polite smile but didn't otherwise respond, certain it wasn't a serious invite. He wondered if the Elizabeth part was true. Was Cheseret trying to establish territory? It flashed through Jack's buzzing head that the whole encounter was some kind of weird game being played on him by Cheseret and Elizabeth, but he couldn't think of what it might be and dismissed the thought as paranoia. He knew his perception and judgment had been off lately. He made another effort, more blunt than earlier, to get a sense of the situation from Cheseret: "Did you just meet Elizabeth?" But Cheseret made like his English failed him and turned abruptly to talk with one of his Italian guy friends. Elizabeth was talking and laughing with her girlfriend. Jack floundered. He badly wanted to re-establish the thrilling electricity with the luscious Elizabeth and wasn't ready to throw in the towel yet.

Eventually, though, he began to tire of hanging out with the group of strangers. He wanted to be alone with Elizabeth, stand close to her, fumble-communicate without the noise and other people around. He was positive he could rekindle the excitement. He wanted to feel her lips with his, run his hands over her body, press against her. See where it led. It was her last night there, which could work in his favor, but also meant it was now or never. He knew that returning to the dance floor would be a letdown. What they should do was step outside, just the two of them, into the cool hush of the night. But he couldn't quite manage to make it happen. His earlier elation was leaking. Fortunately, the club was closing. He hadn't realized how late it was. Typical of the speed—one moment it was eleven, the next it was four in the morning. Or sometimes the sun was coming up, time to seek the safety of the crypt.

The group drifted outside onto the otherwise quiet street, along with other departing revelers. The party atmosphere dissipated quickly. The night air felt good on Jack's skin, in his lungs. Cheseret issued a general invitation to come back to his hotel. Jack demurred, hoping Elizabeth would too. The arousal between them had felt so good. How could she not want to at least toy with it a bit more? But she wouldn't let him catch her eyes, and showed no sign of breaking away. Cheseret was talking to her, and with a laugh gave her a hug and light kiss on the lips. Jack slipped away down a side street.

He walked along the narrow crooked back lanes in the darkness and silence, frustrated and disappointed. He caught sight of a flitting movement out of the corner of his eye. He felt certain it was a person or maybe a dog, but when he looked, nothing. He kept walking, now sensing the shadow people lurking behind him in the murky spots along the deserted street. He hadn't ever seen them clearly, but he envisioned them wearing monk-like robes with droopy cowls covering their heads. And when he looked inside the hoods where their faces should be, all he saw was infinite blackness, not even glowing eyes. He reassured himself that they were optical illusions and walked on as if they weren't there.

As to Elizabeth, he knew full well that's the way it went sometimes. You never knew. In trying to pick up enticing young women, things always had the potential to go south, sometimes in just a moment. Or maybe there had never been a chance in the first place. Sometimes women were just flexing their allure, seeing how it was working. Having fun flirting, getting some reinforcement. With Elizabeth, though, it had felt so much on the verge, especially with the carefree hedonism of summer in the Greek islands in the air, which he knew from pleasurable past experience could have a potent liberating effect.

What a shame, he thought. *Comes with the territory, though. If you're going to chase women, and choose your targets based on looks and sexiness, you're going to crash and burn sometimes. It's a given. Accepting that is key to the successful conquests.*

Oh, well. It was fun there for a while. Other times, the flirtation and titillation might have been enough. But tonight it wasn't. *I wanted more. I wanted the full conquistador experience tonight. Yes, in the privacy of my own mind, I'm allowed to have absurd thoughts like that.*

He felt a devastating crash coming on like a twenty-foot wave rushing at him.

Jenkins and Timmy were asleep when he slipped into the dark apartment. He thought about going into the bathroom and jerking off but didn't feel up to it. Instead, he went out onto the balcony and sat in one of the two chairs. The moon wasn't out, only a few stars. Dark nothingness took the place of the landscape in front of him.

His spirit slammed brutally into the invisible wall of rocks that seemed to always be lying in wait for him these days.

He woke the next afternoon soaked in sweat, terribly rested. His sleep had been shallow and intermittent. He was lucky he'd managed to get any at all, could have easily lain awake all night. Later in the day, if he managed to abstain, it'd be a very different story—he'd fall out and sleep like the dead.

Timmy's bed was made, and he heard no sounds from the other room. The bedroom was stifling; it was an interior space with no windows. The main room would be less so, but not by much. The heat wave that had hit when he was in Athens had settled in for the summer. The shrill buzz of the cicadas pierced even the inside walls, jabbing needles in his brain. He got up and shuffled into the other room where there was natural light, alleviating his feeling of death warmed over. Neither of his flatmates was in the apartment or out on the balcony. He opened the small fridge, and to his relief found a two-liter plastic bottle of cold water about a third full. He drained it and felt marginally better. A glimmer of a dream from his uneasy sleep floated on the periphery of his mind—he'd been walking in a fantastical forest with an abnormal variety of trees—banyans with multiple trunks, cashew trees with twenty-foot branches a foot off the ground for the entire length, towering stalks with high canopies, garlanded at the bottom with beards of moss, vines swarming down, giant ferns clogging the woodland floor. The jungle-like forest was both wonderful and frightening. The glimpse of a dream slipped back into foggy depths. He closed his eyes, tried to relax and pull it back up. But it was gone. *Par for the course.*

He went over and flopped down on the couch, which Jenkins folded up each morning. On the floor at one end was Jenkins' duffel, always padlocked when he wasn't around. Jack had pulled it from the storage space in the belly of the bus they'd taken from Athens to Pelios and had been surprised how heavy it was.

Jack noticed the shackle of the lock was short of being fully inserted by a fraction of an inch. He knew right away he was going to look. He leaned over, pulled the lock open, and removed it. Dragged the bag over in front of him, stood it up and pulled the opening wide.

The top half was empty, collapsed into folds. Jenkins had put some clothes and other stuff in one of the dresser drawers, which Jack had looked through on their second day there. Inside the duffel, the top layer consisted of neatly folded clothes for colder weather. A pair of beat-up work boots. A large Bowie knife in a leather leg-sheath; he extracted it, revealing a nasty-looking back edge of quarter-inch teeth. A canteen attached to an olive drab web belt. Two paperbacks: *For Whom the Bell Tolls*, and Nietzsche's *Beyond Good and Evil*. "Christ," Jack said out loud with a laugh. The first dozen pages of the Nietzsche were heavily underlined, and after that nothing. There were a couple of loose photos inside the cover of the Hemingway—one of Jenkins sitting on the deck of a large pleasure boat with a can of Estrella in his hand; the other of a woman with light brown skin wearing jeans, sandals, and a billowy untucked white shirt. Pretty. Jack wondered whether she was Tunisian, from his time there.

A pair of heavily used work gloves, stiff as cardboard. Papers, documents—work related; nothing of interest. A large bulky object wrapped in a torn piece of cloth with dark grease stains on it. He unwrapped it.

Jesus fucking Christ! Jack stared. Disassembled parts of an automatic rifle.

There were a few more items in the bottom: several boxes of ammunition, a heavy steel gray pistol wrapped in a greasy pillowcase.

This was way outside of Jack's realm of experience. He sat and thought. And thought some more, absorbing the information, trying to discern what it meant. What it might mean for him.

He carefully repacked the duffel as he'd found it, and locked it.

That evening, with some artificial assistance, he made his way through the cluster of cubist buildings and pristine streets to the Oasis, the harbor-front café where Timmy worked. She wasn't there, but Jenkins was, sitting at a table drinking Carlsberg. Jack told him about the fiasco the night before with Elizabeth. As he finished, who came walking along the harbor front but the young woman herself, with her dark-haired girlfriend.

"Elizabeth," Jack called out, and got up and jogged over to them.

It turned out their hotel room had been robbed the night before, and a lot of things stolen, including cash. They had to stay another day while money was wired to them from Athens. Cheseret had gone back to Rome.

It's on, Jack thought with an inner burst of excitement. The girls were on their way to Pure, another of the seemingly endless bars and clubs on the island. They invited him to join them, and he readily agreed. He went over to Jenkins, told him what had happened, and invited him to join them, knowing he wouldn't.

"You go ahead," Jenkins said with a grin. "I'm gonna sit here and enjoy the night air."

As the evening unfolded, the dark-haired girl did most of the talking, getting running input from Elizabeth in Greek. It turned out they'd met Cheser, as they called him, and his group of friends, on the first day of their holiday, and they'd all wound up hanging out together for their vacations. Cheser had immediately formed a crush on Elizabeth and courted her in a stagey way, being charming and entertaining. While she liked him and was amused by his antics, she wasn't interested in him in that way. He was very effeminate, and the girls thought he was "bee-sexual," which might be why he'd invited Jack to Rome. The night before, it hadn't seemed right to go off with Jack, since it was supposed to their last night all together, and Cheser purported to be so infatuated. They'd been surprised and disappointed when Jack had disappeared.

Jack and the girls wound up at Borzoi again later that night, drinking and dancing. Jack laid off the speed for the evening, which took more willpower than expected and resulted in him getting more drunk than usual. At some point, he and Elizabeth went outside for some air, and almost right away went into a clench against a wall in the shadow of some thick overhanging vines, kissing with intense passion. She had wonderfully pliant lips, and it was fantastically sensual to feel them with his own. They kissed hungrily, then lazily, then hungrily again. It was as if the language barrier and not being able to really communicate heightened their desire, as it burst forth in the dark, inflaming them, their bodies melding together.

They both wanted to go somewhere more private. Elizabeth went back inside to talk to her friend. She came back out and indicated they could go to her hotel. On their way through the rustic town, he learned that her father worked as a "pee-lot."

Soon, they were entwined on her bed, lips feeling lips again, mostly unclothed, caressing. Her youthful body was wondrous—firm and supple. The tone of her buttocks and breasts was a pleasure just to feel. She writhed to his touch. He pushed aside her G-string and found she was fully wet.

But Jack couldn't get a hard-on. Not for the life of him. Until a few months ago, he'd never thought about getting hard. It just happened, always. But it wasn't happening now. He'd been rock hard in the shadows outside the club. He'd had to strain not to come in his jeans. But now that she was ready to be taken, it wouldn't happen. She tried to help, but her efforts were futile. Soon the pressure and embarrassment made it out of the question.

He stood up, and with no smoothness or delicacy, pulled on his pants, grabbed his shirt and sneakers, and slipped out the door. She still lay on her bed, mostly naked, confusion and hurt showing on her face. He made no effort to be kind or human. All he felt was utter humiliation and an overpowering desire to get away.

He walked through the dark, empty streets again, stunned. The ghost people, or whatever they were called, walked behind him, making faint sibilant sounds. There were two that were taller than the others, who seemed to be the leaders, and they walked only a few feet back, each behind one of his shoulders. He tried to ignore them but didn't have much success, staying acutely conscious of them all the way back to the apartment.

He'd had trouble sexually a few times with Timmy but had managed to produce some firmness and perform. But tonight he'd been completely limp—nothing happening at all. It could be the speed, or maybe the alcohol from the evening. Christ, though, he was only twenty-eight.

My cock, he thought. *My goddamn cock. Chasing women is what I do. It's who I am, a big part of it. It's how I relate to women, however fucked up that is. How I live with being so detached. It gives me contact. My cock is wired directly to my brain. It functioning is key to me getting the ego-juice I need. My cock is my shaft. I plunge with it, impale. Fill, thrill. It's my tool, my instrument. It's how I consummate my conquests. What if I can't get it up anymore? Will worrying about it make it worse?*

This is a disaster. I have to have my sexuality. I'll be a husk of a person without it.

Timmy was waiting on tables at the Oasis. It was early evening and the Oasis was filling up, along with the other outdoor cafés and tavernas along the waterfront. A wide promenade ran in front of the row of establishments, between the outdoor tables and the picture-postcard harbor, and people actually promenaded there in the evenings while the customers seated at the venues watched. It was an integral part of the village's social life during the summer, and to a lesser extent during the spring and fall, which some Aegean aficionados said were the best times to experience the special essence of the islands.

The sun was still a half hour from falling behind the hills of Kyros, but the promenading had already begun. Timmy liked the older village couples best, out for their evening constitutionals. They dressed with casual formality. The grizzled mahogany brown husbands wore freshly pressed baggy trousers with pleats, and short-sleeved button-down shirts, some hanging loose, others tucked in showing wide leather belts. The wives, mostly thick in the waist, wore colorful summer dresses going well below the knees, and shoes with low thick heels. The old couples walked slowly, arm in arm, stopping here and there to talk with other villagers. This was the heart of their social life—coming out in the evenings after a day's work and mingling with their fellow islanders. They took little notice of the tourists. This was their island, their life, and they were content with it. They gave off no yearning to live elsewhere or have other lives. They manifested a quality of abiding over the years, seemed to have reached an understanding with life, not to question it. To Timmy, they seemed very lucky.

As she took an order from some German girls, Jenkins walked up and sat down at one of the empty tables. Timmy was surprised to find she was glad to see him, and went over to his table next.

"Hi. Want a Carlsberg?"

"Yeah," he said, surprised she knew. He was in a good mood.

She returned with his beer and lingered.

"Jesus, you stink," she said with a laugh. She noticed a bad gash on one of his hands, oozing blood. "Christ, what have you been doing?"

He took a long drink of beer, with obvious satisfaction. "I've been out fishing." He smiled.

"What do you mean?"

"I started coming down to watch the fishermen in the evenings—pulling up their boats, laying their nets out to dry, smashing octopus against the rocks, tenderizing them, I think. After a few days, I asked one of them if I could go out with him one morning. Made it clear I wasn't looking to get paid. At first, they didn't get it. But then one of the old guys said for me to meet him there the next morning at half past five. I'm pretty sure he didn't think I'd show.

"But I did. And I went out with him and another guy, and we fished. The other guy wasn't very friendly until he understood I wasn't trying to take his job. He laughed when he realized I was working for free. Laughed and laughed. Couldn't get over it. Couldn't believe anybody would do the back-breaking work without getting paid.

"At the end of the day, we delivered our catch to the old guy's regular customers, a bunch of tavernas and housewives. A woman, who I think is the old guy's daughter, sold what we had left from a cart. The old guy, Stavros, took me and the other guy to drink retsina at a café in a part of town I'd never been in. I don't really like the stuff, but I drank it to be friendly. Got a bit drunk with them. Stavros kept slapping me on the shoulder and saying stuff in Greek to everybody there.

"Today was my third time out. I've gone out every other day." He took another long swig.

"Why are you doing it?"

"Oh, something to do. I don't much like sitting around doing nothing. And fishing is one of the oldest, most basic forms of work. A hard way to make a living. It's all some of these guys have ever known. Goes back in some families for generations. There's something . . . real about it. It has a . . . a bedrock kind of value . . . I don't know." He trailed off and shook his head.

The owner of the Oasis called Timmy's name and nodded firmly toward some waiting customers. "Oh, shit," she said. "I've got to get back to work. Talk to you later."

CHAPTER 6

Jack pushed the tree branches aside, careful not to break any. One of the branches almost poked him in the eye, and he had a fleeting thought of the disastrous effect that would have had on his day. Sweat trickled down his face and the sides of his torso.

He and Jenkins were walking on the other side of the island's ridge-top, where they couldn't be seen from the white villa. The sun's location indicated they were headed south. Jack craved more speed, but he was already having trouble keeping Jenkins in sight among the trees in front of him, and it wasn't a good time to stop.

The shadow people were scattered in the woods behind him, moving soundlessly. They seemed to glide. He'd never been quite sure whether their feet touched the ground or not.

* * *

Mid-afternoon, broiling, like a sauna. Timmy was at work wiping off tables and straightening chairs. She was wearing cutoff jeans and a sleeveless white T that would have provided glimpses of her pert breasts if she hadn't been wearing a bikini underneath. Her skin was golden brown, a shade that would have been impressive even back in Sydney, with its thirty-nine beaches. There was only a smattering of customers at the Oasis, sitting in the shade of the striped awning, brown and cream-colored, looking overheated and tired, some bored. The neighboring cafés and restaurants had no patrons at all.

As Timmy knew, traveling wasn't for everyone, especially if you weren't doing it in luxury. If you weren't insulated from the harsher elements, travel could be grueling, uncomfortable, and confusing. One big hassle, including foul-ups you knew were a possibility but couldn't avoid entirely, plus completely unforeseen problems—lost luggage, flat tire, delayed flight, missed flight, workers' strike, injury, theft, getting lost, hurricane, volcanic eruption—the list went on and on. Murphy's Law was at least ten times more applicable when you were on the road, especially when navigating unfamiliar territory. Luxury insulated travelers from the inconveniences of globe-trotting in any number of ways: comfortable plane seats, private train compartments, rental cars, drivers, guides, spacious hotel rooms, air conditioning that worked, swimming pools, lounge chairs with umbrellas and waiters, a good concierge, and the rest of the trained-to-please staff at a first-class hotel. And above all, ample funds. Without these things, or most of them, in order for traveling to be worth the trouble, you really had to get it, genuinely feel the special pleasure and fulfillment that came from experiencing foreign lands and cultures. You had to have a genuine curiosity about life and the world, and the ability to enjoy the simple experience of being interested in what you encountered.

Timmy liked working in bars and cafés, especially in vacation spots. *Who wouldn't?* was how she saw it. It was basically hanging out in pretty places with fun social scenes. An assortment of interesting people were regularly passing through—backpackers, bad boy charmers, privileged types from worlds alien to her, intense Scorpios, easygoing Pisces, loners, unique characters who lent atmosphere to a watering hole by just sitting at the bar. And if you stayed in a remote locale for an extended time, you fell into a pleasing slower rhythm, a stark contrast to the frenzy of metropolises full of competitive go-getters.

The work was easy. Timmy hadn't gone to university and had no great ambitions, no fervent longings. She just had the urge to get away from Australia and see the world, find out a bit more about herself. She had a feeling that she hadn't fully blossomed yet as a person.

She had a delightful uncomplicated quality that hipsters and earthy guys the world over were drawn to, and even a few straight-laced types who were secret dreamers or were put off by polished women. She looked fantastic in jeans and a T-shirt, very feminine, and could glam up impressively when she chose. She wasn't elegant but had a special charm all of her own. The Greek guys loved her, especially her wavy golden hair and bright blue eyes.

In the course of her travels before Jack came along, when the yacht she worked on was in port, on occasion she would sight a young man with an intriguing quality and a face that was strongly attractive in an unusual way—never the classically handsome for her—and she would feel lust and wonder what his story was. Sometimes she gave into it. She'd had a few promiscuous periods in her life. Now she'd been with Jack for three months—Jack the flaming asshole. *Not for much longer*, she thought. She didn't even know why she was still with him at this point, other than inertia and having a traveling companion of sorts.

She was a stray, in some ways a typical Aussie young woman—beach loving, fun, and flaxen-haired—out for her extended stretch of world traveling, as a lot of young adults from down under did before settling down. But it wasn't just any young woman who ventured out into the big bad world on her own, even among Australians. Originally, a girlfriend had been supposed to come with her, but she'd bottled out a week before departure. Timmy hadn't considered not going for even a moment.

She'd always felt in a weird way that Australia wasn't her true home. Like maybe at birth she'd somehow popped out into the wrong place, maybe even the wrong family. Like maybe there was someplace else out there that was her natural home. Her parents had done her some serious harm. Her family life hadn't been the way it was supposed to be.

Her downfall was she was drawn to the wrong kind of guy. But she had something special to give, especially if she received real warmth and affection in return.

Timmy started out her travels by flying to London in November of 1988, planning to stay there awhile and then cross the channel to the continent and explore the incredible array of cultures packed so closely together. She wasn't in London two months, though, bartending in a pub in Shepherds Bush, when a regular there, one of her fans, told her of an opportunity to be a crew member on an old-school sailing yacht going around the Indian Ocean and neighboring seas. She had some basic sailing skills, which she'd picked up from being raised in Sydney with its gorgeous gargantuan harbor. She applied for a position, and was asked in for an interview.

The yacht owners were a wealthy English couple in their fifties who exuded a privileged health and vigor. Three of their friends were joining them on the voyage—another couple and a guy. The boat was being transported to Singapore where they would embark. It was going to be a long trip in close quarters, and they wanted a capable crew they were comfortable with. They seemed well organized and competent. They'd gone on lengthy sailing trips before; this was their most ambitious yet. They seemed nice enough, though extremely posh, which made Timmy uncomfortable, but she hid that. There was a modest salary in addition to room and board and the life experience.

She didn't mind changing her plans. Her intention from the outset had been to see where things led her, and the expression "cast your fate to the winds" had always resonated with her. Being from Australia, she'd have much preferred the Mediterranean or the Caribbean, but the Indian Ocean wasn't without appeal. They offered her a position, and she figured, *What the hell?*

Singapore—the ultra-modern city-state with almost no trace left of its colonial glory days, a shame to Timmy's way of thinking. Strikingly clean and, as best as she could tell, all business. Her employers put her up at the legendary Raffles hotel, in a tiny room originally intended for servants, and thus fitting.

They launched with a champagne toast and headed south to Java and Bali—lush jungle-like vegetation, terraced hillsides of deep saturated green, gentle natives, expats searching for something, and some who were just lost souls. Then up through the Strait of Malacca to Phuket and Koh Samui, where the Thai island life was still exotic and unspoiled.

The food had flavors that were revelatory and cost very little. Koh Samui in particular struck her as a great place for extended stay, as she later learned Jack had done.

Then across the Bay of Bengal to the deep water harbor of Colombo in Sri Lanka, full of hulking container ships, a tricky port to navigate in. There was fighting going on in the north of the island nation, with the colorfully named Tamil Tigers, but Timmy felt no threat exploring the ancient southern city. The natives smiled all the time and shook their heads when they meant yes, regularly making for amusing confusion. The country had at different times been a colony of Portugal, Holland, and England, and between that and having been on international trade routes for over two thousand years, it was strikingly multicultural. She loved the resulting blends and hybrids that had made their way into the culture—a red London double-decker bus alongside a herd of cattle, social clubs that could have easily been in the English countryside, Dutch/Indonesian cuisine, markets full of bright colors, informal cricket matches on patches of open land. She and another crew member, a nice enough guy, rented a scooter and drove into the countryside, through sprawling tea plantations and cinnamon orchards. The latter had a pungent tangy fragrance like nothing she'd ever smelled.

Then onto the Maldives with its romantic boutique hotels, each with its own little island paradise. The yacht owners generously had the crew join them for a sumptuous lunch at one of them. She fantasized about spending a few weeks there with a beautiful man she was in love with and who loved her back. She hadn't yet experienced in her life a deep, profound love, and naturally wondered whether that was something in the cards for her.

The western coast of India—hippies, affluent bohemians, tropical poverty, decorous temples falling down, being reclaimed by vegetation. "The jungle always comes back," a creepy guy with blond dreads said to her at a particularly decrepit temple.

The whole journey was a spectacular, once-in-a-lifetime experience. The places they landed were full of alien ways and cultural spice, and several had natural beauty that inspired awe and stirred the soul.

There was the social side as well. They anchored with other boats in various harbors and secluded idyllic bays reachable only by water. Boating people were very sociable. It was odd—people who went on long boat trips said they were looking for peace and quiet, but they were always dying to see other people and hobnob whenever they got the chance. For one leg of the trip, they sailed with another big yacht—people the owners bonded with in one of the bays accessible only by boat.

Timmy got along with everybody on board but didn't become close with anyone. She had a couple of flings in the ports when she had time ashore, went to some bars and restaurants that were the real deal, thick with atmosphere, usually from another era, though occasionally strikingly modern.

There were, of course, long stretches of open sea. Distances in that part of the world were much farther than people realized. Basic activities like boat maintenance, food preparation, keeping the cramped quarters below deck clean and organized, all took on extra importance and became primary activities, rather than incidental tasks slotted into the rest of life. Meals were always a big event. Life on board was reduced to simplicity.

She felt the inevitable overwhelming feeling of insignificance, of being a tiny speck in the universe. And she got a full sense of the mighty power of the sea, ever present, even when calm, and the brawn of mother nature. Even a hint of weather was enough to get everyone's attention. They were so far from anywhere. They were fortunate, though, and only ran into a few medium-sized storms, which they still took seriously.

The ubiquitous endless waves soaked into her—the rocking motion, hypnotic sounds, rippling visuals, all minutely ever changing, having a lulling effect down to the very bottom of her soul. Tons of solitude, time for thinking, an area in which Timmy had only recently begun to explore her full capacity. She could feel how traveling was making her more of a thinking person, and was glad that was somewhere in her, beginning to bloom.

Her spirit became serene. She had moments when she felt like nothing could ever bother her again.

There was boredom and loneliness too, of course. They were never in port for long, and she didn't get a proper chance to explore the places they stopped. And island paradises, as beautiful as they were, were all a bit the same. The endless socializing of boating people in port could get tiresome as well. Alcoholism was rampant, not so much on the open sea, but certainly when they were in the harbors and towns. She was good at fending off drunks without making them feel too bad.

She acquired a sense of what people meant when they referred to "the sadness of the tropics." It had something to do with the swamp-like lassitude brought on by the constant sweltering humidity. Life in tropical countries was different. She couldn't put it into words, but she could feel that people who spent their lives between the latitudes of Capricorn and Cancer had a different view of life, of mankind.

Somewhere in the Indian Ocean, the husband of the guest couple on board decided he wanted to have sex with Timmy, which became troublesome for her. The guest who was a single guy was gay and had always been cordial with her.

One glorious afternoon, they were anchored in the scenic harbor of Baie Sainte Anne in the Seychelles, near the main dock. Timmy lay out on deck in a bikini, and lifted her head to watch the ferry come in from La Digue, a nearby island that gave new meaning to the term "sleepy," where the primary mode of transport was still the ox-drawn cart. She watched the passengers walk down the gangway and noticed among the stragglers a lanky beautiful young man with long brown wind-blown hair. He was wearing aviator sunglasses and had a beat-up black canvas bag hanging from his shoulder. She stood up, rose on her toes and stretched, and dove gracefully into the indigo bay.

When she surfaced, he was standing on the dock watching her. She treaded water and smiled at him. Having already noted her rangy figure, he was struck by her startlingly blue eyes. He gave her a slight smile, looked around at the island's green hills, then back at her, still moving her hands in the water to stay afloat. He smiled more broadly. Dropped his bag and sunglasses on the dock, pulled his T-shirt over his head, kicked off his shabby canvas sneakers, and with only his baggy linen cargo shorts still on, dove in. He said later, intending to be humorous, that seeing her tread water had made him think that was a good way of describing his life.

Maybe she should have known right away he was an asshole. But she didn't. Or maybe she did a little and ignored it. Within a day, she bade her employers and boatmates a poorly received good-bye. She would have preferred not to tattle on the bothersome husband, but felt guilty about leaving the owners in the lurch and wanted to give them a solid reason they'd have trouble arguing with. So she told them what had happened, concluding, "I'm just not comfortable on the boat anymore."

And off she went with Jack.

Early July 1989. Kyros.

Late one night, Jack was extremely wired, stretched tight to the point of breaking, figuratively bouncing off the walls, and he felt an overwhelming urge to spill. Talk—about anything, lots of things, at length. Some specifics zoomed around his brain, but the compulsion related to just about any topic, as if spouting words, verbal noises, was all that mattered, not their subject. And while he was at it, he wanted to down some whiskey. He didn't want to freak out some stranger, or worse yet, make the guy think he'd found a new friend. So, he headed for the Kentavros and was vastly relieved to find Jenkins sitting on his usual barstool there.

"Doctor Wu" was playing over the sound system: "Just when I spent the last piaster I could borrow." *God, I love that song*, Jack thought. The sweet, haunting sax came in, and he shivered with pleasure. His jaw ached from clenching.

He didn't bother with opening pleasantries, and launched into a gush of words as soon as he ordered a Dewar's on the rocks: "You know, a lot of people daydream about having adventures. All the Walter Mittys of this world. They sit around all day long leading their humdrum lives, imagining exciting exploits that'd take them out of their spirit-killing existences. Simple stuff like finding a gym bag full of cash or a suitcase full of cocaine. They sit at their desk or wherever they work and figure out how they'd handle it. They think how they'd be smart and not tell anybody about this incredible thing that's happened to them, even though they'd be dying to tell everybody in sight. If it's coke, maybe they figure out how they'd turn it into cash, even though they barely know anyone anymore who gets high, and haven't the slightest idea where to begin. Or if it's a bag of money, they think how they'd be disciplined and not spend any of it for a good chunk of time, avoid drawing attention to themselves. Whatever the daydream is, they work out all the details of how they'd pull the thing off.

"Every guy thinks about stuff like this at one time or another. Because it's an inevitable thought, and it's fun to think about."

Jenkins had no idea who Walter Mitty was but was following the general thrust of Jack's harangue, which continued nonstop.

"Maybe they daydream about the big score, an opportunity falling in their lap to easily steal a lot of money. Like a safe gets mistakenly left open with a stack of cash in it. Or maybe the person's job is paying the bills for some company, and he figures out a way to make payments into a bank account he sets up without anybody catching on for a nice long time. Or they get left alone in a room for a few minutes with a bunch of uncut diamonds lying out on a table. For people involved in shady behavior, uncut diamonds are the most desirable form of wealth, better than cash sometimes. Uncut diamonds are easy to transport, small but with a high value, relatively liquid, and almost impossible to trace. Anyway, all this crazy stuff that has about a one in a billion chance of happening in real life, but that doesn't stop guys from dreaming."

Jack took a sip of whiskey, then spun off again. "Maybe they need to get the money out of the country, so they figure out how they'd go about doing that. Or maybe they need to disappear before they get found out or the people whose stuff it is figure out who has it, so they work out how they'd go to ground, maybe leave the country, get a fake identity so it'd be extra hard to find them. But stuff like that isn't so easy. It's not like it is in the movies. I mean, in real life, how the hell do you get a fake passport that will actually pass muster? Where do you find an expert forger? With the special paper and the right ink, the right stamps?

"Or maybe the Walter Mitty type needs a gun for some part of his imaginary caper. How do you get one that can't be traced to you? For that matter, how do you get a gun at all? Most people wouldn't know how to get a gun other than going through a whole official rigmarole, or driving to some redneck state where they sell guns over the counter, and even then you probably have to show a driver's license or something. In the movies, people get untraceable guns like they're buying a pack of cigarettes. It's ridiculous.

"And why do people daydream about all this stuff, work out all the details for things that are never going to happen? Because people are bored out of their fucking minds. And they're desperate for excitement.

But these incredible flukes never happen in real life. And people just go on with their dreary lives, with their screams of quiet desperation."

It's a good thing it's me sitting here, thought Jenkins. *This would get tired real quick for most people. It's okay as bar talk, but he goes on . . .*

"The Walter Mittys of this world, their favorite films are ones like *Casablanca*, full of intrigue and danger—a nightclub in Morocco during World War II, with the country run by Nazis and French collaborators, and the path of true love runs up against a chance to help good triumph over evil. Classic story.

"'*What in heaven's name brought you to Casablanca?*'" Jack mimicked dialogue from the film, trying to effect a French accent, then responded in a voice meant to sound like Bogart: "'My health, I came to Casablanca for the waters.' '*The waters? What waters? We're in the desert.*' 'I was misinformed.'"

Jenkins was lost. Jack was babbling, as far as he was concerned. Not that he cared all that much whether he followed Jack's rants, especially when he was as messed up as this.

"Or the literary folks," Jack rambled onward, "they have the place they like to call 'Greeneland'—an exotic third-world country where worldly expats live out their personal dramas against a backdrop of some kind of major turmoil, like a revolution or war, which wreaks havoc on the expats' personal lives. People read books like *The Comedians* or *The Quiet American* and imagine themselves in situations like that, having a real adventure. But in the real world, they'll never live in a third-world country or experience true excitement. All they'll ever do is read books and watch movies. And daydream. You can't build a career and make decent money, have a family, buy a house, and in the same lifetime run a failing hotel in Haiti during the Papa Doc years, or work as a foreign correspondent in Saigon as the French colonial era comes crashing down. To even have a chance of genuine adventure, the real thing, you've got to take chances in life and accept the strong possibility that you'll wind up in some dead-end existence. Or maybe you accept a life of drudgery up front, like soldiering or working on a ship, in the hope it leads to something exciting. And even then, you've still got to be willing to wind up being nowhere, having a nothing life. Being one of life's losers."

Jack slid off his stool and went to the bathroom to bolster himself.

Why book readers might think Greenland was an exciting place was beyond Jenkins. He wasn't sure, but thought it was just a big, cold island in the north Atlantic, where hardly anyone lived.

Jack returned sniffling, and Jenkins said, "Jack, you're just going on and on, making the same point about fifty different ways. What the hell are you getting at?"

"I'm talking about actually doing something to get some real excitement in my life, actually making it happen, instead of just being one of these ineffectual losers who are all talk, never seize the day." Despite his assertive response, Jack actually wasn't sure that was what he'd been getting at. He might have lost the thread, he wasn't sure. But in the face of Jenkins' challenge, this was the thread he blithely picked up and went with, not knowing whether it tied in with what he'd been jabbering about before. With his brain going two hundred miles an hour and barely holding the road, he had little idea if the segue made sense, and wasn't stopping to check. "I mean," he zoomed on, "what is real excitement? Smuggling drugs? Running guns? Going to war? Robbing a bank? Those are the things they make movies about, write novels about. But I'm not about to do any of those things.

"I've already done my share of drug smuggling, if only for my own consumption. I came within a whisker a few months back of getting my chest blown apart by some psycho with a shotgun. I've been robbed at gunpoint trying to score—the guy put the muzzle of his gun right up against my thigh to make it clear he'd pull the trigger if I made him. I might wind up with a hole in my leg, but he wasn't going to be facing a murder rap. And I've been beat up. Bad. I'm lousy at fighting. The days of the amateur big-time drug smuggler, like Mr. Nice and the guy in *Snowblind*, are long gone. They came and went during a half dozen years in the late sixties, early seventies. Then the pros took over. If an amateur were to try serious drug smuggling today, he'd get ripped off and chopped into pieces before he got out of the gate.

"And gun running. What I can never figure out is how big-time arms dealers get to be big-time arms dealers. How do you move in circles like that? Where do you get the weapons? In quantity? Especially the heavy-duty stuff, like RPGs? And where do you find people who want to buy them? Who've got the cash? How do you handle the transport? Not get caught, not get ripped off? Killed?"

Jenkins could have shed some light on this subject, but didn't.

"I can just see myself driving around Mogadishu in some beat-up car," Jack sped on, "rolling down the window and saying, 'Pssst, man. Wanna buy some Kalashnikovs?' Jesus, it's a joke to even think about it."

Jack's glass was empty, and after making sure the bartender wasn't looking, he took a quick swig from his flask. Jenkins marveled at his ability to talk, or rather babble. Jenkins didn't think he'd ever said half as much himself in one sitting.

"And war," Jack raced on. "There's a book called *Dispatches*, written by a war correspondent who was in Viet Nam. He talks about the addictive nature of war—how once you've been in a battle zone with your life seriously at risk, regular life just feels flat and lifeless."

"Yeah, right," said Jenkins with annoyed sarcasm. "Regular life feels safe and sound. It's a good thing. It's what any sane person wants."

Jack careened onward. "Soldiering. Even if I'd been willing to enlist when I was younger, it would've been almost a hundred percent certain all I would've ever got to do would've been drudge work. Maybe I'd have wound up peeling potatoes in the mess hall. Real exciting. Wouldn't that have been funny? Most soldiers never come close to seeing any action. America hasn't been at war for over fifteen years, if you don't count Granada, which was nothing, over in a few weeks. Not to mention how absurd it would've been to think I could handle the training and getting ordered around. I wouldn't have lasted day one at boot camp."

Jack had a lost and confused look on his face. "Maybe I should've been a cop . . ." he muttered, and trailed off. Scratching the scar on his knee, he got distracted by the song that was playing. "Wicked jam," he mumbled. Then he perked up and said, "Which brings us around to you. I know you've had the real deal, genuine adventure. I can tell. So, tell me. What have you gotten up to?"

"None of your goddamn business."

"Come on. Have you ever worked as a mercenary?" Jack was nervous about asking this, but gave himself a shove and did it.

Jenkins ignored him.

"Come on."

"Listen. I served in the US Army and learned it's not much better than a loony bin. Now shut up. I'm not talking about stuff that don't need talking about. I'm telling you, don't say another word. In fact, stop talking entirely. I'm sick of listening to you and your . . . I only listen 'cause I . . . Your bullshit passes the time. But we ain't talking any more right now. Understand?"

Jack went silent. He had a palpable sense that if he pushed it any further right then, Jenkins would really hit him. Hard. Jack hadn't known many people you couldn't push past the lines they drew in the sand at least once or twice. But his gut told him Jenkins was one of them.

CHAPTER 7

Jack felt disoriented. They were walking downhill through a pine forest toward the odious villa, but he wasn't completely sure what they were doing. Or rather, he knew what they were doing but was having trouble remembering why and how. His brain felt fuzzy, the antithesis of the preternatural sense of clarity he'd experienced that morning.

He looked up and saw a weathered board nailed to a tree. Painted on it was "The Waiting Room," which added to his confusion. He remembered reading about the sign somewhere. Jenkins walked past it without looking.

* * *

Early March 1989. The Seychelles.

Timmy and Jack took the ferry from Mahé, the big island where most of the locals lived, to Praslin, the next largest of the group, where the placid tranquility of the Seychelles was complete. They stayed there for five weeks, which turned out to be their only truly good time together. For the equivalent of about three dollars a day in local rupees, they rented from a Creole-speaking native a one-room structure made of cinder blocks, with a wooden floor, a corrugated tin roof, and a couple of cots. It had a doorway with no door, and empty openings for windows, neither of which mattered, as theft on the island was virtually nonexistent. The glorified shack was part of a cluster of similar dwellings scattered haphazardly among a grove of trees on the southern coast, not quite rising to the level of a village. The other dwellings were homes of natives, squat nut-brown people with round faces, reflecting a mix of French and African ancestry.

There was an outhouse and an outdoor shower, the latter consisting of an oil drum on a raised wooden platform that filled with rainwater and was operated by pulling a knotted rope. Their landlord was one of their neighbors, and he was happy to have found travelers willing to accept such a rustic accommodation.

It was sunny almost every day, and each night there was a torrential rain of exceptionally large drops that made a din on the tin roof so loud Jack and Timmy had to shout to make themselves heard inside the shack, which made them laugh. The nights were warm, and sometimes they'd step outside into the deluge, which was like standing under a waterfall—exhilarating and making them laugh all the more.

Their existence was what people who had dropped out in a more developed country would have called "going whole hog" and adopting the full-bore simple life. There was a surprisingly wide variety of fruit trees that nobody seemed to own, and Jack and Timmy plucked and picked from the ground whatever they wanted. They especially liked the star fruit, which Timmy had never had before. The islanders had some garden plots where they grew vegetables, which they sold to Jack and Timmy for next to nothing. And of course there were the endless fresh fish from the bountiful sea, caught by native men who went out daily in skiffs. The local women liked Timmy and were happy to show her how to make elaborately seasoned local dishes.

Most days, Timmy and Jack walked a half mile along a dirt path through dense, lush trees to a secluded mile-long arc of sand called Anse Lazio. The beach was perfection and could easily have been used as a "slice of paradise" setting in a Hollywood movie.

Coconuts usually lay on the sand under the palm trees that lined the back of the beach. They had thick husks, and Timmy didn't realize what they were at first. Jack explained the husk was called the exocarp and was removed from the ones sold in shops and markets. "They're not even nuts," he said. "They're fruit." The local makeshift tool used to open them was a board with a spike sticking through one end, and there were always a few lying around. Timmy and Jack would first drink the refreshing milk, then eat the crunchy white meat—"the endocarp," he said.

Sometimes they just sat at the back of the powdery crescent in the shade of the trees and stared out at the twenty or so different shades of blue and green of the Indian Ocean, from bright clear turquoise near the shore to midnight blue farthest away, and all the hues in between. Occasionally, they bantered over whether a particular strip of water had a tint that qualified as unique and what name to give it—teal, cerulean, foam green . . .

They had sex three or four times a week, not as often as Timmy would've liked, but she wasn't overly fussed about it. They hung out regularly in local bars with thatched roofs, where the patrons were mostly islanders. On the beach near one of them, a grizzled old man sold fresh lobsters grilled over an open wood fire, served with a special tangy sauce for which he was known. They sometimes smoked hash that Timmy had acquired in Goa.

Jack seemed almost normal to Timmy, almost happy, though not quite. She couldn't quite get a fix on him, what he was really like. She wasn't sure what to make of his moods and his occasionally strange manner—in addition to bouts of being withdrawn, he had bursts of being manic, suddenly becoming wildly enthusiastic about one thing or another. And he had poor people skills, often being rude and putting people off. She quickly took on the role of being his social buffer.

He didn't hide from her that he was doing speed, but did it only in the evenings, and not every one. She didn't know it, but his intake on Praslin represented a much-needed cutback from a recent phase of massive drug abuse. She didn't partake of the meth, which she associated with people who were skanky and haggard, living on the margins of society. When Jack was speeding, he became less present, as if his person slipped behind a screen. He gravitated to the natives and drank more often from his cherished flask.

Even before they left the Seychelles, she sensed he was holding back. He was nice to her and interesting to talk to. He could talk about real stuff—the mind-boggling way life dealt out its cards, how everybody was weird in their own unique way—but always at a distance, never as if he were talking about himself. Before long, she reluctantly recognized he wasn't giving her real warmth and affection. He rarely looked her directly in the eyes, missing just slightly, steering his gaze to some other part of her face, like her cheeks or lips. And he didn't often smile.

She wondered what was wrong with him but didn't come right out and ask. He seemed very much inside himself, and his face oddly lacked expressiveness at times. Later, it occurred to her that maybe he hadn't been holding back. Maybe that's all there was.

Timmy could have fallen in love with him if he'd acted differently, but she knew she could say that about a number of guys. Her alky father, who she didn't like to think about, said annoyingly often, "If a frog had wings, it wouldn't bump its ass so much."

When she let her guard down, her natural way was to be sweet and affectionate with her man. She was powerfully physically attracted to Jack. He was sexy without making any effort—lanky, a good height, with angles and contours in all the right places, especially his gaunt face, which caught shadows in the concave spots. He carried himself upright and yet with a hint of a slouch, which gave off a certain erotic suggestiveness. His hair seemed to be permanently wind-blown, and she loved the blond streaks in it. His body felt amazing when he was naked and pressed up against her—firm and sinewy, with the ins and outs that had such a stirring effect on her.

They often lingered at the beach in the evenings to watch the blazing sun slide down behind the horizon—her favorite time of day. One evening, as the fiery yellow sphere hung low in the sky, he surprised her in the extreme by telling her about his childhood in great detail. He did it in a strange way, though. His speech became highly mannered, different than his usual relaxed speech patterns. His manner of talking changed so much it was as if another person had taken possession of him.

"As a child, my family's house was in a gated community in Darien, Connecticut, though I was off at school or camp most of the time. On a street called Delafield Island Road, lined with mansions and elaborately sculpted landscapes—man-made ponds, imported trees, flagstone paths in the woods. Our house was at the end of the road, with an enormous lawn in back sloping down to the Sound. There was a boathouse with a wooden cabin cruiser and a sailboat. I was required to learn how to sail, both at home and at summer camp, though I can count on one hand the number of times I went sailing with my father. It came in handy later on, though.

"The house was built for President Polk, the eleventh president of the United States, who I understand historians give a decent rating to as leader of the country.

"We had dog kennels, which I've always suspected was a manifestation of my mother's pretentions. All cocker spaniels, beautiful dogs, but very temperamental, difficult to handle. They were looked after by our gardener, Toby, who I was quite fond of and spent much of my time with during my limited stays at the family residence. His primary responsibility was taking care of my mother's two-acre rose garden, with its curlicue brick paths. It's amazing the frivolous things people will spend large amounts of money on.

"My father was a trusts and estates lawyer at a Wall Street firm, a name partner. Page, Fowler and Ferris. His clients included the estates of two men who had been wealthy industrialists and philanthropists. I think that having those clients played a key role in making him feel he was a success in life.

"My mother was a stately woman. Nothing more, nothing less. An active member of the Daughters of the American Revolution, descended from a Virginia tidewater family of French Huguenots. They'd been driven from France by Catholic persecution toward the end of the seventeenth century and probably had to leave much of their wealth behind, but they quickly became American aristocracy, such as it was.

"I'm pretty sure I was a mistake. I don't think my parents wanted children. And when you're wealthy, you can go a long way toward insulating yourself from the burden of offspring—nannies, boarding schools, summer camps. You barely have to see your progeny. And when we did all sleep under the same roof, we didn't exactly have what people would call quality time. Most days, my mother started drinking wine at lunchtime and continued discreetly throughout the day. She was usually looped by early evening. My father holed up in his library most of his time at home. Floor-to-ceiling bookshelves on three walls, with only well-bound books on display, and a large bay window overlooking the Sound. I remember being curious about one book in particular with a thought-provoking title—*The Art of Thinking*—but I wasn't allowed to take it off the shelf. The only furnishings were a Persian rug and a pair of leather club chairs with reading lamps. The room always struck me as the perfect refuge for my father.

"As best as I could tell, he was a misanthrope. Though maybe Bukowski's formulation is closer to the mark: 'It's not that I don't like people. I'm just happier when they're not around.' As my father never seemed happy, though, maybe a more accurate way to put it for him would have been: 'I'm just less unhappy when they're not around.'

"Mother and Father were killed in an automobile crash when they drove up to Maine for the first time for visiting day at my summer camp. It happened less than a mile before they arrived. It was my fifth year there, and I have no idea what prompted them to come up that year. Horrible decision.

"I was twelve at the time, and from there on in I was pretty much on my own. My parents weren't on speaking terms with any of our relatives, and I hadn't met any of them to my knowledge. They didn't reach out. My father never seemed to come from a family, as far as I could tell. My mother met him when he was at Columbia and she was at Barnard. She must have realized early on that his background wasn't distinguished, and more or less blocked it out. There may have been more to it, but not that I know of. In any event, after they were married, they managed to fall out with everyone on her side of the family. I've never been clear what the acrimony was about, but I always suspected it had to do with money."

A swathe of gold stretched toward Timmy and Jack across the placid evening ocean as the blinding yellow-pink ball began to drop below the horizon.

"Much to my surprise and chagrin, when my parents had their fatal collision with the big oak at the fork in the road, it turned out they'd been living on fumes for the past few years. They had tons of debt, and most of their assets had been used as collateral for loans. Apparently, my father's practice fell off dramatically as management of the two big estates was taken over by the charitable foundations they funded, and he hadn't managed to attract new clients of major substance. It may well have been luck that landed him the two big fish in the first place. And it may have been good my parents died when they did, as I don't think they would have dealt well at all with impoverishment.

"It was then I learned that a trust had been established for me when I was born by my mother's father, who died when I was one year old and I don't think ever met me. The trust could only be used to cover my expenses, and was paying for me to attend the various child-rearing asylums I was shipped off to most of the time. At least I hadn't been a financial burden to my parents. Barclays Bank served as trustee via a revolving cast of executives over the years. It was made clear to me that I needn't be concerned about money, that my bills would continue to be paid. Fortunately, none of the bank executives have ever tried to give me life advice or anything like that. I stopped going to summer camp after one more year, but continued at boarding school until graduation. I could see the benefits of a decent education. It's good to understand what smart people are talking about. And it's good to understand the way the world works, how things got to be the way they are.

"Anyway, after I graduated, I started the life I have now, which isn't easy to characterize. Sometimes I refer to it as inquisitive loitering. I've dabbled on the spectrum of human activity from what passes these days as the bohemian life to out-and-out debauchery. And I've skidded completely off the rails a few times. Early on, I acquired a profound distaste for the privileged life, so I've never been drawn to a conventionally wealthy lifestyle.

"Unfortunately I don't have a lot of money. Or maybe fortunately. But at least I've never had to get a job, which is good because I don't like to work. I might well be a homeless person if it weren't for my modest stipend. You know what they say about poor people being crazy, and rich people eccentric."

She didn't, but understood. *What a sad, sad life*, she thought. *Though he definitely doesn't bring out the sympathy in people. I wonder if it's all true?*

"As you've gathered," he said, shifting to a conclusory tone, "I move around a lot. I don't actually have what you would call a home address. What little mail I get is sent 'in care of Barclays Bank.' I have to travel cheaply, but I'm okay with that. I prefer it in some ways. So far, so good. Only problem is I'm getting sick of being on the road, and I'm a stone-cold drug addict, which costs money and presents problems I'll only be able to ignore for so long. Eventually, the trust isn't going to provide me with enough money to get by. But we'll see what condition I'm in when the time comes, and whether it matters."

He stopped talking, and the stranger who had possessed him slipped back into some hidden place inside him. His tone of voice had stayed fairly matter-of-fact throughout, showing only an occasional tinge of bitterness or sarcasm.

Timmy soon came to realize that this mannered way of speaking was one of his ways of belittling the world of privilege and money. And conveying his deep-seated loathing for his parents and everything they stood for.

The strange thing was that Jack actually liked Timmy, in his way, to the extent he was capable. He enjoyed her good nature, especially her tolerant undemanding ways. And he appreciated her being an essentially happy person, in the way that people full of misery know that hanging out with a person tuned in to the brighter side of life can ease their raging despair. He thought Timmy was great, or rather he could tell that most people they encountered thought she was great, and he was glad to have her as a traveling partner.

But he was bored by almost everything and everybody, most of all himself. He'd come to a point where he saw life as something you wandered through, with small doses of direction mixed in with a lot of aimlessness, and occupied yourself as best as you could without taking on anything arduous or tedious. Timmy's efforts to enable her budding affection for him to bloom only had the effect of making him withdraw.

His speed intake rose sharply as they got ready to leave the heavenly isle. The two of them had managed to have a cocoon-like existence there, insulated largely from his normal suffering due to the hell of life and other people.

They flew to Dar es Salaam, a big bustling city, hot like an oven. Jack wasn't in the mood for it, and after one night in a hostel they made their way to the port and caught a ferry to Zanzibar. An interesting island—the inhabitants were almost all black or Arab, very few tourists.

"So, this is what it feels like to be a stranger in a strange land," Jack mused out loud. It was a large island, with plenty of regions to explore.

The people were predominantly Swahili and extremely dark skinned, a deep purplish black. There were leftover buildings and other remnants from when the island had been a British protectorate, but otherwise it was very native in character. There were numerous beach areas, and they settled down in a magnificent one up north called Unguja. Jack spent much of his time there in basic bars with the locals, some of whom spoke pidgin English. Timmy wasn't comfortable in the native taverns and didn't join in.

She was interested in real travel like this—exploring authentic places off the beaten track—but this was a bit outside her comfort zone. She found some amazing reefs and snorkeled regularly, drifting facedown in the preposterously luminous sea, mesmerized by the ultra-vivid-colored fish darting and slinking. She took pleasure in the way the submerged activity shut out the world and shifted her brain into a state of being focused solely on the visuals passing in front of her mask. She was particularly fascinated by the way the schools of fish swam in perfect unison, every one of them abruptly changing course in the same instant without any sign as to how they coordinated. She saw barracudas floating in shallow depths without moving for long periods, their long jaws hanging open, displaying rows of jagged teeth; they paid her no mind. By far her favorite underwater sight were the spellbinding pink and orange jellyfish wafting through the crystal clear water with otherworldly grace, their mushroom cap bodies undulating in slow motion and tentacles trailing below. She never tired of watching them.

Twice she was lucky enough to see schools of dolphins up close. She remembered with an inward smile the popular science fiction novel where all the dolphins had mysteriously disappeared from the planet Earth and had left a lighthearted message for the humans, clueless that Earth was designated for demolition to make way for a new intergalactic highway: "So long and thanks for all the fish."

Above the surface, she was mesmerized by schools of flying fish zooming through the air for intervals of fifteen feet and more, again and again.

She tried to convince Jack to come see it all, especially the spectral jellyfish with their extraordinary translucent colors and enchanting movements. She was sure he'd love it. But he wouldn't. He'd shifted into a new mode. She started to feel lonely, and she was a person generally okay in her own company. She also began to be slightly concerned about the mental stability of her traveling companion. Wondered how much obligation or responsibility she had.

She'd felt mildly threatened when they'd first arrived in Unguja, and the feeling gradually increased. A blond white woman was like a freak of nature there, and groups of leering unsavory types loitered daily in their spots of choice and made lewd remarks in Swahili as she walked by. Not that she understood the language, but the tenor of the comments was impossible to misinterpret.

One night, Jack got into a bar fight and was stabbed with a knife. He was extremely drunk and never clear as to exactly what triggered the foul play. All he remembered was he'd heard two natives utter the word "blond" numerous times, and then seen them simulate fucking an imaginary woman bent over a bar table. Exactly how this led to the knifing he couldn't say.

He had the serendipitous luck of a fuck-up. The puncture was in his left side below the rib cage where there was an abundance of organs, but none of them was harmed. A local doctor cleaned and stitched the wound. Jack was rather proud of it, but Timmy was quite firm it was time to move on. Jack acquiesced, having had his fill of the place anyway.

Back on mainland Africa, they journeyed by train and bus to the coast of Kenya, where a short ferry ride took them to the island of Lamu. The overall trip challenged even their fairly high tolerance for discomfort and inconvenience. For one leg of the journey, they hired a dilapidated car along with its owner as driver, and one of the wheels fell off completely, leading Jack to wonder what the outcome would have been had they been going more than ten miles an hour. They got stuck in a shantytown for a very long day waiting for a bus, in the midst of a shockingly desolate landscape, which did their heads in as the day wore on. The shoulder strap on Jack's bag broke, a real pain in the ass, as one of the handles was already broken, the type of small thing that could drive you mad when traveling. From inside a train stopped for an inexplicably long time at a rural station, they saw a ragtag band of men brandishing guns and machetes with too much relish for comfort. Jack and Timmy had no idea who they were or what was on their minds. Jack realized for the umpteenth time that he was in more danger traveling with Timmy than on his own.

Africa seemed like a completely lost cause, left way behind by the rest of the world, with large regions of seemingly intractable, abysmal living standards. *It must be horrible to be an average African with no way out at all*, thought Jack. And this was in Tanzania and Kenya, where there were some areas with passable living conditions.

When they got to Lamu, as Jack had said, there There was an ultra-hip hotel called the Peponi, a hodgepodge of bright white Arabic-looking buildings on a sandy bay. It was quite luxurious in a rustic way, and they couldn't afford to stay there. They took a room at a local guesthouse and hung out at the Peponi bar most afternoons and evenings.

Jack was in his element, still with a good supply of his demonic fuel. There were always interesting travelers passing through and hanging out—Germans, English, French, Italians, Scandinavians—drinking and talking endlessly, comparing their fabulous lives of exotic expeditions. And most of them were keen to prattle and yammer with Jack, or rather listen to him prattle and yammer. He was wired out of his mind during most of their time there, enabling him to drink all comers under the table. He was always the last man standing. He was viewed as a real character at the Peponi, which satisfied one of his lesser ambitions. The management got used to him and soon treated him as an honored guest, even letting him continue to run up a bar bill after it was clear it wasn't going to be fully settled.

He created versions of himself Timmy knew had to be fictitious, blending them with reality. One evening, he told a bunch of Germans about working as a seaman on one of the mammoth container ships plying the trade routes in the South China Sea. "Once, we watched from the bridge as Malay pirates boarded the far end of the ship, and we let them loot a couple of containers without making any effort to stop them. No point in confronting men with AK-47s over a bunch of TVs and air conditioners. The captain claimed twenty-five thousand dollars was taken from the ship's safe, which the pirates never came close to.

No question it went in his pocket. Ships always carry a good amount of cash to deal with matters that can only be handled that way, and it was probably covered by insurance."

He told people about hanging out in Aden and chewing Qat with the natives. "They kept saying how good it made them feel, but I barely felt a thing, less than strong marijuana. It was bullshit. The Yemenites need to get themselves some drugs with oomph."

One evening, he told a bunch of admiring French how he'd worked as a roadie for the Talking Heads on the Stop Making Sense tour. "I worked at the shows that were taped for the concert film. The opening song every night was 'Psycho Killer,' and at the end, the guy on the mixing board made the tick-tock drum sound like machine gun fire, and David Byrne did a perfect imitation of Jean-Paul Belmondo staggering around to his death in the final scene of *Breathless*." The French ate it up.

He told a group of Dutch and Swedish: "I went to Woodstock when I was fifteen. Watched Richie Havens open the festival with 'Freedom.' I was soaked to the skin for three days straight. Lost the guy I hitchhiked there with on my first day there. Dropped acid for the first time with some kids from Brooklyn. Sat down at any campfire I felt like. "

Timmy knew this had to be fiction. Jack had been eight years old in 1969. And it probably occurred to a few of his boozed-up listeners that he didn't look thirty-five.

He repeatedly told people he'd met Dylan, and in the course of talking to him had asked how many kids he had. "He said, 'Some.'"

Other times, he went on diatribes about terrorism and his ideas about something he called benevolent terrorism, usually causing him to lose some of his audience. But there were always some drunks who'd talk about anything endlessly.

She didn't know if people believed his stories, but the topics were usually sufficiently out of the ordinary to make for interesting bar conversation, and he wasn't without skills as a raconteur, though he did tend to ramble on. He was the type of character people wanted to meet at the Peponi, so they wanted to believe his offbeat ravings. When she asked him about his fabrications, he didn't seem to see anything dubious or objectionable about them. "Hey, that's part of who I am," he said. "I tell stories. Reality and fiction, sometimes mixed together. There's plenty of reality in fiction, and plenty of fiction in reality. I take on different personas, some of them made up, but they're still part of me. What comes out on any given occasion depends on my mood."

———

From Lamu, they took several buses down the coast to Mombasa and flew to Khartoum, where the Blue Nile meets the White Nile. Jack found a hotel for them near the juncture of the famous rivers, run by a jovial expat Greek family. Jack and Timmy went to the Omduran Souk where they were constantly pestered by kids begging or trying to steer them to one merchant or another. The urchins were like fleas and became tiresome. Timmy and Jack retreated to a more upscale neighborhood, where the harassment for some reason simply didn't occur.

Jack splurged and took Timmy to a fancy restaurant called Al Housh in a lovely old townhouse with an interior courtyard, where on arrival they were pleasantly surprised to be escorted to the ornate rooftop terrace for pre-dinner cocktails. They stared out at the vast sprawling city and its legendary rivers. At dinner, Jack ordered the pigeon, and insisted Timmy try it. She had to admit the uniquely seasoned dish was quite savory. They asked the waiter what the sauce was, but he courteously declined to divulge the ingredients, saying it was a secret recipe for which competitors would pay large sums of money. This sounded fanciful but was a nice atmospheric touch. The only negative of the evening was that the restaurant was in a neighborhood that had become so dangerous they had to be delivered right to the door by taxi and picked up there afterward.

Jack was frustrated by how difficult it was to get an alcoholic drink in the Muslim country, and the absence of women in the cafés. "Who wants to hang out with all guys?" he complained.

He was surprisingly well-informed about a terrorism incident that had occurred in Khartoum several years earlier. The Palestinian terrorist group Black September had taken ten hostages at the Saudi Embassy, including the US ambassador and deputy ambassador, who were there for a meeting. Both US diplomats were executed, shot in the back of the head. It was widely believed Yasser Arafat was behind it, but it was never proved, allowing him to retain a veneer of legitimacy.

"The terrorists surrendered," said Jack. "Two of them were just let go. The other six were sentenced to only seven years in prison, and three of them escaped in the first few months, with almost no effort made to track them down.

"A fucking travesty. If I'd been in charge, I'd have assumed the hostages were all goners and stormed the embassy. Killed every last one of the terrorists. I wouldn't even have given them a chance to surrender to the probably sympathetic authorities."

Jack also talked with awe about the way the Israelis had handled Operation Entebbe. Over a decade earlier, he explained, Palestinian terrorists had highjacked an airliner out of Tel Aviv that had about a hundred Israeli passengers on it and forced the pilots to fly it to Entebbe airport in Uganda. They released the other passengers but held the Israelis hostage. A hundred Israeli commandos swooped down in the middle of the night, killed all the terrorists, and saved almost all the hostages.

He talked with particular venom about "fucking Idi Amin, the dictator of Uganda at the time, who fully lived up to his reputation as a monster. He personally welcomed the terrorists and had his troops join in the fight against the Israeli commandos, killing their commander.

"One of the hostages was sick and even the terrorists allowed her to be taken to a local hospital. But after the successful rescue, Amin had her dragged from her bed and killed.

"And Kenya allowed the Israeli planes to refuel en route to Uganda at one of their airports, and as revenge Amin slaughtered hundreds of Kenyans living in Uganda, and sent agents who assassinated the Kenyan minister who talked the Kenyan president into cooperating.

"The Israelis killed forty-five of Amin's soldiers and wiped out his air force, destroying thirty planes. Showed him what real warriors are like."

Timmy acknowledged that the Israeli operation sounded impressive, but he seemed overly preoccupied with the events, and she didn't want to encourage his interest.

"Now Amin's living in the lap of luxury in Saudi Arabia," Jack concluded. "Another fucking outrage."

Timmy couldn't figure out why Jack knew so much about these incidents, or why he cared so much. When she asked, he responded, "There are really bad people in the world. Evil in their essential nature. People like Hitler, and another Nazi named Heydrich, who came up with the Final Solution and was one of the most intrinsically cruel and vicious of the Nazis. These people should be killed as soon as their fundamental evil starts to gain footing in their societies. And the assassin would be doing the world an enormous favor. He'd be completely justified, like the heroes who parachuted into Czechoslovakia and killed Heydrich with a bomb. They were completely in the right, had no reason to feel any guilt. And what they did was exciting and important. The honorable people of the world knew they'd done the right thing."

She accepted what he said about there being bad people in the world, but he lost her when he got to the "exciting" part, which made it sound like he was talking about some kind of boyhood adventure. Plus he didn't strike her as someone who cared all that much about good and evil, though she was mistaken on that score.

Jack did have an ethical scheme of sorts. It didn't really hold up under scrutiny, but he had one all the same. His thinking was murky, and he made sure it was never subjected to rigorous analysis.

He knew his desire for adventure and excitement was laughably romanticized, and didn't even begin to take into account the dangers arising from truly perilous action in real life. The appalling example of real-world carnage that always came to mind when he thought of such horrors was from the most baseless of wars, World War I: he had a vision of literally tens of thousands of men clambering up stepladders out of the trenches to near-certain death, unleashed almost immediately by ferocious inescapable machine gun fire and artillery. He always wondered how the generals had managed to induce their men to commit mass suicide for no discernible reason. Jack wouldn't have done it. He'd have deserted. And would have known with absolute certainty that his decision was the only sane one.

Nevertheless, he managed to push such misgivings and flaws in his thinking into hidden pockets of his brain, and clung to the belief that if he channeled his perverse quest for excitement in the direction of doing the right thing, the madness of his desires would somehow be circumvented. That was the catchphrase he hung onto and repeated over and over again in his head—doing the right thing. He believed that people with honor always knew in their gut what the right thing was, regardless of intellectual arguments for and against, and that enlightened mankind had a collective sense of justice. Right-thinking people, deep down, knew what the right thing was, a tautology of sorts, but it worked for Jack. An exciting exploit that passed this test was, for him, readily excusable and justifiable, despite any possible resulting harm.

As a corollary, he'd developed an intense loathing for people who got their excitement from doing evil. As he'd suggested to Jenkins on the strikingly clear morning on the open ferry deck, getting your thrills from doing bad things was a scam, like shooting ducks in a barrel. Doing bad was by definition exciting. It was too easy.

But to engage in adventure that involved doing the right thing, that seemed extraordinary to him, a thrill that could justify a wide range of behavior and enable a person to fully embrace the experience, especially if it was done for something that crucially mattered to society.

Jack ignored all the holes in this scheme of things, and it worked for him.

They went next to Cairo and Alexandria, at last getting close to the "holy Med," as Jack referred to it. He was repulsed by all the garbage in the Egyptian cities—piles of it lining, even blocking, the streets, masses of it filling up the spaces between buildings, rooftops covered with hills of it. He couldn't believe the cities had once contained one of the world's most advanced cultures.

They were out walking on their second day there when they came on a bearded man wearing the traditional turban and long robe, standing on a wooden platform talking with vehemence to a group of mostly young men, seemingly passersby who'd stopped to listen. Jack walked over and stood about twenty feet behind the gathering, observing though he couldn't understand what the man was saying. Timmy hung back. The speaker soon spotted Jack and addressed him directly, switching to surprisingly good English: "You are American, am I right?"

The listeners turned and stared at Jack, who didn't react.

"I studied in your country for two years," the orator said. "Boston, Massachusetts. I know you believe in the separation of church and state. But you are wrong. There can be no separation of church and state. They are one and the same. We are creating a caliphate where the laws of Islam will be the laws of government, where the religion of Mohammad will govern all men.

"You are an infidel. Without God. Thus you are doomed. The end of your time is coming. We will eliminate all the infidels. Even if it takes five thousand years. We will never give up. That is why we will prevail. *Allahu Akbar.*"

Jack spit on the dusty street and walked away. There was an angry rumbling from the crowd, and Timmy was afraid they were going to come after him, but the man on the platform said something in Arabic, and when the crowd looked back his way, he extended his hands and lowered them slowly. He watched Jack walk away with a look that seemed to exude an all-knowing certainty. Or maybe it was just plain hatred.

"That's the Muslim Brotherhood," said Jack. "They've been around since the 1920s, over sixty years now, trying to create a country ruled by Muslim law so they can make everybody live by their medieval beliefs. They're allowed to operate openly here, and they're gaining momentum. They're the biggest threat to mankind in the world today, and the US is barely even aware of them. Not that I care much about the US, but those guys are true fanatics. They literally believe we are the devil. And they'll never give up. That's their ultimate strength, which we don't get. We focus our energies on the imbeciles in Europe pretending not to be bourgeois and playing at being terrorists. They're not the real thing. Nobody's doing anything about the real threat.

"Benevolent terrorism is the answer. Take care of business like the Israelis do. They're done with taking chances with the way the world treats them. 'Never again,' they say. And they mean it, to the bottom of their souls. They don't give a fuck what anybody else says. And they back it up. I say, let the people with scruples be the hindmost. Scruples are for the dainty, and they're no match for evil. You've got to fight evil with evil, believe you me."

Again, Timmy followed him up to a point, but then he started sounding crazed to her. This was clearly a hot button issue for him, though, and she left it alone.

His aversion to Egypt increased his eagerness to get to the Greek islands, which seemed to represent some kind of haven for him. He said it was where he went when he needed to recover from his incessant travel, to recharge his weary spirit.

"Going back to New York always feels like defeat for me," he said. "The Greek islands are where I go in my head when I get really down. It gives me a lift to just think about being there. Actually being there is going to be great. I'm going to clean up my act, get my head straight. You're going to love it."

The next night, after an almost inedible dinner in a cafeteria-style restaurant in Alexandria, they returned to their budget-priced hotel. They shared a double bed, and as they lay there, he started to caress one of her breasts. She pushed his hand away, and he accepted it.

They never had sex again. He never tried. They never talked about it.

He seemed fine to continue traveling with her, though she wasn't sure it was such a great idea for her to stick with him. But she was looking forward to the Greek islands, both from his rapturous talk and the glowing things so many other people said. Timmy knew he'd be an excellent guide, show her the best things. He knew how to extract the sweetest elements from travel, the intangible hard-to-find kind, even if he didn't get much pleasure from them himself anymore.

They took a ferry to Crete, and another to Athens.

———————————

Mid-July 1989. Kyros. Jenkins was sitting by himself at a table at the Oasis when Timmy arrived for her evening shift. She came over and chatted with him for a few minutes. A nearby table of rambunctious Greek boys showed obvious appreciation for her. "Year of the Cat" was playing on the outdoor speakers.

"So, come on," said Timmy, "what's the story? Tell me really, why are you hanging out with Jack?"

"You been hanging out with him yourself awhile."

"Yeah, well," she said, like it didn't mean much.

"Jack's all right," he said. "Most of the people I'm around are half brain-dead, one way or another. Jack can be entertaining. He's different. Sometimes I wonder what it's like being him. Not that it looks like fun. He sure as hell ain't having a good time. But still, I wonder how things seem from where he stands. What his experience is like, seeing the world the way he does." He ran his fingers over his mustache.

"He's fucked up, sure. But only half as much as he makes out to be. And he can be a jerk, sure, but he's okay to drink with. He's got a good line of bullshit. Goes on a bit, 'specially when he's cranked up. But I'm in between projects right now. I got time."

CHAPTER 8

Jack began to see figures flitting in the pine forest, hiding behind trees. They seemed to be the shadow people, but there were a lot more than he'd ever seen, and they were armed with weird-looking guns—sort of retro-futuristic pistols and machine guns, as from a graphic novel. And somehow their gray robes kept morphing into gray military uniforms, switching back and forth, like an image printed on special plastic that changed when you viewed it from different angles.

The most horrible aspect of the hallucinations, which he knew they had to be, was that the ghost people had somehow become the enemy. It wasn't as if he'd ever felt they were on his side, but somehow they'd been conjoined with him, trying to coax him into their netherworld, join them on their diabolical path. Now they seemed to be in league against him. He wondered if they were going to start shooting their cartoonish-looking weapons. Would their bullets do the usual damage?

Jenkins seized hold of Jack's head like a vice, one hand on either side. His incensed face appeared squarely in front of Jack's, a few inches away, and commanded in a fierce whisper, "Snap out of it. Now."

* * *

Late one night, a few years earlier, in Manhattan's foul-smelling meat-packing district—around three-thirty in the morning—Jack sat at the counter of an all-night diner trying to get down some scrambled eggs, with limited success. It was a place where after a certain hour, a disparate throng of inglorious patrons gathered—taxi drivers, hookers, trannie hookers, seedy club kids, punk rockers, drag queens, and the occasional odd-looking contingents in formal attire. Cops regularly stopped in for coffee, surveying the crowd.

On the second stool to Jack's right sat a down-and-out-looking young woman, nursing a coffee. She wore a dress that looked like it came from a thrift shop, threadbare and old-fashioned with a patterned print from another era, the hem falling down in a couple of places. Her worn-looking shoes had thick heels and straps with little buckles. Her brown hair hung limply. No makeup to speak of.

She started mumbling. Jack assumed she was talking to herself and ignored it. But the volume gradually increased, and he started to catch words and phrases: "Lipstick . . ." "And then he said to me . . ." "It was raining . . ."

The jukebox chimed in: "Billy's got cleats on his boots . . ."

She plausibly could have been talking to Jack or the flamboyant waiter wearing a turban, standing between them on the other side of the counter, but it didn't seem like that. The nonsense she was babbling slowly became more distinct: "I told him not to . . ." "Sally was always saying things like that . . ." "I don't know . . ."

Jack glanced at the counterman, with his one dangling blue earring. No reaction there. Not sure why, but Jack turned toward her slightly. She began spewing phrases more audibly, words pouring forth: "Bunch of Okies . . ." "Didn't think it would be so cold . . ." "The rats. My lord, the size of 'em . . ." "I wish I could talk to Darren . . ." "Out of the question . . ."

A number of other customers had turned to listen. Her jabbering picked up speed, the words becoming a blur. Pretty soon, it wasn't even worth trying to follow her. Louder, faster, never a pause. She was clearly under the influence of a powerful compulsion. The words came tumbling out because they had to, regardless of whether they made any sense or who might hear.

The jukebox: "No, she won't take a train . . ."

More snatches from the addled young woman: "Everybody has stories . . ." "People get old, don't mean they stop wanting . . ." "I don't know why I do it. Wish I could say . . ." "Then he told me to . . ."

It gushed. For what had to be seven or eight minutes, utterly bizarre, faster and faster. Jack couldn't tell how she managed to take a breath. Then, in short order, she ran out of steam—slowed down, returned to mumbling, lapsed into silence, and looked down at her coffee cup.

There was a smattering of applause from various tables. Jack heard regular conversation from the far end of the diner where people hadn't been paying attention. To his surprise, he had a feeling like someone should go over to her, make some contact, some small gesture, maybe touch her lightly on the shoulder. But he knew it wasn't going to be him. The counterman refilled her cup.

It was a striking thing to witness, and probably made a bigger impact on Jack than other listeners because he'd been there himself. Methamphetamine had sent him on innumerable free-wheeling talking jags, sometimes with people he'd just met. Possessed like that, he often could barely maintain his train of thought, lurching from one subject to another. Other times, he was coherent but his blather went on and on. He was aware of how weirdly he was behaving, that he should stop talking, but couldn't. He had no choice but to keep jabbering, hoping people would put up with it. His synapses snapped, crackled, and popped like a downed power line whipping around in the street. If nobody aggressively told him to shut up or stop talking shit, jarring him to a halt, he just had to wait until his engine ran down and the cascading mix of sense and nonsense finally ran out.

He'd made a fool of himself plenty of times, but that was a side effect of his drug of choice, and he was willing to live with it.

He often subjected Jenkins to word torrents. Jenkins didn't seem to mind all that much. He had a certain patience with Jack, a forbearance that others didn't. Usually the two of them were at a bar, but sometimes they sat out on their apartment balcony. Jack would take a trip to the bathroom—he was inexplicably fastidious about doing his drugs in private—and on return start spewing verbal diarrhea on one or more topics. Sometimes Jenkins paid attention; sometimes not.

One night, they were drinking at the Kentavros, with Tom Waits growling over the sound system, and Jack launched into a harangue: "Everyone gets bored. Nobody likes it." He took a quick sip of whiskey. "And everybody looks for ways to avoid boredom. Maybe they're not aware of it, 'cause most people don't have any idea what's going on, not even in their own lives. But they do it, they try to avoid boredom. And that's when they engage in the pursuit of being interested.

"Most people are lucky. The simple shit works for them. TV. Fucking TV. The average guy'll sit around in front of a TV for all of his spare time and be completely content. He's got images he can stare at and sounds he can listen to, and he doesn't much care what they are.

"When you're young, school helps pass the time in a low-grade way, but it makes for more boredom than it relieves. Same thing with work later on. School and work can engage you occasionally, so they're not a hundred percent boring. They're diluted boredom, which I suppose is better than sitting alone in a jail cell with nothing to distract you. That's the real deal, full-bore boredom, the shit that makes you climb walls. The seconds go tick, tick, tick, slow and steady, and you can't imagine how you're ever going to get through the next hour, much less the whole goddamn day.

"Some people don't mind boredom. They *like* to veg out, sit around all day long doing nothing, getting stoned or whatever. Slackers. People who aren't really living. They flush their days down the toilet, one by one. I figure they must be just waiting for it to be over since they're doing absolutely nothing with their lives. Fucking waste of space.

"Me, boredom drives me crazy. I can't stand it. I have to escape it. And the way to escape boredom is to be interested. If you're interested, you're not bored, by definition. Plain and simple."

Jack glanced at Jenkins to see if he was listening. Couldn't tell. A Queen song came on. Jack hated Queen, especially Freddie Mercury's shrill voice.

"Anyway," he rambled on, "since being interested keeps you from being bored, the thing to do is figure out how to be interested as much of the time as possible. I've tried every form of being interested there is. Reading, sports, chasing women, sex, music, drugs, chess, backgammon. I thought acid was the answer for a while, like a lot of people. For more than just boredom, I suppose. Until one night I wound up thinking rats were eating my face and I was setting the alarm clock for every five minutes 'cause I was convinced beyond a shadow of a doubt that if I fell asleep, I'd never wake up again. Wound up in a psych ward, full of thorazine. Man, that shit'll bring you back to boring reality real goddamn fast.

"I even tried painting, believe it or not. Problem was, no talent. Big surprise. I tried the nightlife, the low-life. Smack never appealed—all you do is sit around doing nothing, nodding out. Sit on a couch or a park bench, or out on the open deck of the Staten Island Ferry going back and forth endlessly for free, and you're completely content to do absolutely zero all day long. Didn't really work for me, didn't address my needs.

"And then there's travel, the fountain that's supposed to never run dry." Fatigue entered his voice. "But it does. The road is endless, and eventually it gets old and tired.

"I've tried thrill seeking. Motorcycles, parachuting, free-falling, bungee jumping. Hang gliding—running down a ramp off a mountainside into nothing but air, hoping the nylon wings are going to work the way they did on the practice slope. Now that's a moment that gets your full attention. Not one smidgen of boredom left in you."

Jack paused to admire a voluptuous young woman entering the bar with a group, and Jenkins said, "You want to be interested, Jack? Go to war. You'll get interested real goddamn fast when you're in a firefight and every ounce of awareness you have is locked onto the fact you could get killed at any moment. You've got to function with the knowledge that at any moment a bullet could punch a hole in your vitals, and you probably won't even know it happened. You'll just be gone, without even a moment to realize you've been killed, your life is over. Put your life on the line like that and you'll get interested. I guarantee it.

"I'd love to see you with bullets flying. You'd scramble for cover like a crab with the shits. You'd see how much excitement you want then. When you know that motivated, battle-hardened soldiers are out there trying to get you in their sights. That's when you find out who you really are, Jackie boy. And I don't think you'd like what you find."

Jack shrugged. He wasn't insulted. He knew Jenkins was right. He had few illusions about himself. He wasn't brave. He was just plagued by ardent yearnings demanding satisfaction, angry demons.

He went off on a tangent: "I was reading the other day on the beach where this character says, 'The craving to risk death is the last great perversion.' He says that's what causes wars. And war could be avoided if every young man were required at the age of twenty-one to risk death once by a simple roll of the dice. Like Russian roulette."

Jenkins ignored this and said, "I've known plenty of guys like you, Jack. War groupies. They've got their subscriptions to *Soldier of Fortune*, and they go to shooting ranges with their automatic weapons, wear camouflage gear and army boots. A lot of 'em hang out in soldiers' bars, even travel to places near war zones. Saigon was full of guys like that. Cambodia too. And they're all full of shit. You wouldn't want any of 'em with you in a real firefight."

A pall fell over the conversation.

Eventually, Jack started talking again, in a quieter voice. "Some people are just born with boredom hard-wired into them. It's in their genes. And thrown in with that is an inability to tolerate boredom. For people like that, life is just varying degrees of tedium. Torturous sometimes. They're forced by their own nature to continually try to find ways to divert themselves from the monotony of life. And sooner or later, they wind up on a slippery slope where it takes more and more excitement to keep the passing of time from being absolute hell."

"And that's you?"

"Yeah, that's me. Whether you understand it or not."

"And what's your point?"

"What I'm trying to say is that escaping boredom and finding interesting things to do can ultimately lead to serious problems. You need to keep finding new diversions, more effective ones. You need more and more excitement. To the point where you start doing stupid, dangerous shit just to escape the melancholy that boredom breeds in you. And that's when escaping boredom becomes a seriously hazardous activity."

Jenkins said, "Sounds like an easy problem to solve. Just accept that life is going to include some big chunks of boredom, like everyone else does, and get on with things."

"That's just it. I can't do that. I've tried. I get to a point where boredom sends me 'round the bend. It's unbearable. I can't function. If I'm not doing speed, I go into a deep depression. Can't get of bed. Have no psychic energy to deal with people.

"I need excitement. I need to be engaged. That's why I do speed all the time. That's why I'm always on the move. I need to feel like I'm living, even if it means harming myself, like that fight I got into with the assholes. Better to be alive and in pain than deadened and just going through the motions. When I was younger, I felt boredom so intensely I was sad all the time. Deep sadness. It was horrible, especially being a kid. My parents and school didn't have any idea what to do with me, not that they made much effort. I couldn't shake it, not with therapy or medication. I wanted desperately to be able to accept boredom like everyone else does, to not have to constantly be searching for diversions.

"Sometimes, I find myself wishing I could be okay with the feeling that nothing is worth doing, which seems to be my dominant feeling these days. That seems like heaven to me in a way. I know this all sounds crazy to you, or just plain stupid, but it's what I have to deal with. Every goddamn day."

"You might start by laying off the speed a bit," said Jenkins. "That's gotta keep your engine revving. Gotta make it harder to get interested in things, stay interested. Not easier. All that jitteriness and spinning your wheels. Makes it hard to focus on anything."

Jack was leaning forward with his elbows on the bar and buried his face in his hands, dug his fingernails deep into his scalp, hard. After several moments, a drop of blood trickled down his left temple.

He resumed talking, his cadence slowing as his fuel ran low and the exhaustion that was always hovering nearby crept in: "Most people try to find interesting things to do based on the subject matter. It's the subject that's the draw for them. Me, I just want to be interested, period. I don't care what does the trick, as long as I get the sensation of being engaged. I want to feel interested so I can feel alive.

"It's one more way I'm a junkie. I've got to get my fix of excitement and being absorbed, or I go into withdrawal, a tailspin. When boredom sets in, I feel like I'm fading away, disappearing, slowly dying. And these days, I feel that way more and more. I can't seem to find anything that makes me feel really alive anymore."

"I listen to you, Jack," Jenkins said with irritation in his voice, "and I don't know what the hell you're talking about. As far as I can tell, you're just talking about ideas. And ideas aren't doing anything. They're not living, not action. You've got all these ideas worked out in your head, and you get all upset when you can't get your life to fit them. But they're just ideas. They're not things you do. Not eating, shitting, fucking, working. Or drinking." He signaled the bartender for another beer.

"Life's what we got. And you do the best you can with it. And you don't beat yourself up endlessly 'cause you can't live according to some philosophy you've come up with. I get it—life isn't as exciting as you want it to be. It has exciting moments here and there, but most of the time it's just putting one foot in front of the other. And you're gonna have to get used to that.

"You go on and on about how you want thrills, and then you realize that real excitement is a hazardous activity, and you get all concerned and think being okay with boredom would be heaven.

"What the hell do you want? You're not making sense. You're full of shit."

Jack felt his whole person droop. He'd tried hard to convey his troubled feelings and thoughts. But they'd wound up sounding like cerebral jerking off, not real-world concerns. And he'd contradicted himself. He'd failed to get his thoughts across properly.

At the same time, though, he felt like Jenkins did sort of understand what he was trying to say, or at least some of it, but wouldn't admit it out of contrariness and justified annoyance at Jack's bellyaching. *But also, there's a basic way in which he just doesn't get it. He's not made that way.*

It struck Jack, for about the thousandth time, how words were just arbitrary sounds that humans had randomly made up over thousands of years, and were exceptionally clumsy and inadequate for getting thoughts from one person's brain into another's. Communication seemed impossible to accomplish with anything near completeness or precision. *We all just pretend to understand one another, but a lot of the time we don't. We're all isolated on our own little islands of thought, and nobody really understands anybody else.*

Maybe some of the disaffected idiots in the European terrorist groups would understand what I'm trying to get at. Maybe that's the type of person I'm most on the same wavelength with—dilettante anarchists terrorizing their own societies. Pretty pathetic if true.

Jenkins took a long drink of Carlsberg, got foam on his mustache, and wiped it away. "All your ideas, Jack—they're just thoughts your brain makes up, things with . . . with nothing in 'em. They don't do anything. They only exist 'cause you think 'em up. They're less than air." He grabbed at the emptiness in front of him.

"Life is you get up in the morning, you maybe go to work, you eat, you shit, if you're lucky, you have sex with somebody. And that's about it. That's all there is to it. Looking to be interested all the goddamn time is crazy. It's impossible. Life ain't that interesting. So, to hell with your ideas. They're useless. They're only messing up your head, and you're getting worse all the time."

The next day, Jack walked along the curved pretty main street of Kyros Town. The charm of the village charm was lost on him.

Thinking about his conversation with Jenkins, he realized it was hard even for himself to grasp clearly all the thoughts and feelings swirling around inside him. The urges, wants, compulsions—they were elusive, tricky, hard to identify precisely. He felt them, though. And they drove him mercilessly, they ruled him. It occurred to him regularly these days that his brain wasn't working properly, that he was losing his tenuous connection with reality. He knew recently there had been times when he hadn't perceived things correctly—misunderstood something someone was trying to say or do. Maybe his mechanism was broken.

He was on his way back from the beach, salty sweaty and hot, looking forward to a shower in the coldest water the shower in their apartment could produce, mildly cool at most. His omnipresent antennae alerted him to two striking young women about twenty-five yards ahead, sitting on the steps of one of the trendier bars. It was a slick place, not his style, but usually drew plenty of attractive women in the evenings, so he sometimes cleaned up his act and went there. The two women were wearing bikinis with sheer sarongs wrapped around their waists. As he got closer, he saw they were eating dark red grapes from a cluster. One of them was a singular beauty, with a distinct veneer of class and privilege. Blonde and slim. Her face was take-your-breath-away lovely—every feature perfect in a refined way. As he walked by staring, to his surprise she gave him a flirtatious smile.

Christ, he thought, *those ones don't usually show interest in anybody. They sit back and wait for guys to come to them, hardly ever put out inviting vibes. So, what the hell was that?*

Before he turned the corner, he glanced back over his shoulder, and to his astonishment, she was watching him and laughed lightly. He stopped around the corner and stood there. He normally had little inhibition about approaching women, but this situation didn't make sense. Nonetheless, she'd given him too much encouragement to let it pass, so he walked back and said "Hello" with a smile, careful not to expose his missing tooth. He had an appealing smile when he summoned it up. The exceptional beauty broke off a small bunch of grapes and handed it to him. They were juicy and sweet, perfect for his parched throat, with a delicious flavor that made him think he'd never fully appreciated red grapes before.

The beauty was Swedish, the other young woman Danish—dark haired and pretty as well, but overshadowed by her companion. Their English was passable, as with most Scandinavians. The beauty made him think of a Siamese cat—the almond shape of her blue eyes, her long neck, sculpted nose, the languorous way she held herself and regularly shifted her limbs, not so subtly calling attention to herself. She exuded an expectation of admiration. She was a pristine version of her type, of which Jack had encountered a fair sampling in his travels.

After a few minutes of chitchat, he said, "Hey, I'll be down at the Oasis this evening. You guys should come by." They said they would.

He knew there was only a medium chance they'd show, but he had to try. You had to go up to the plate and take your swings to even have a chance. In his experience, the signals you got in the early stages as to whether a woman was seduce-able by you or not were highly unreliable. Some of the most shy, conservatively dressed women shocked you with their brazen abandon, and some of the most provocative, flirtatious women were the biggest letdowns.

"What the world needs is a good nuclear holocaust." Jack was on one of his drug-fueled rants. It was early evening, and he and Jenkins were sitting out on the apartment balcony, feet up on the railing, drinking beer. "Get everybody back to basics. I mean, the way I understand it, if somewhere around sixty nuclear bombs are detonated around the world, the fallout will cause a global nuclear winter, pretty much making life on our planet unlivable, not to mention all the people and cities wiped out in the initial blasts. It'd be like it is in all the post-apocalyptic science fiction, *A Canticle for Leibowitz*, books like that. It'd be like prehistoric times, only worse. Food wouldn't grow, and lots of the rivers and streams would be toxic. There'd be survivors, people in remote places, or maybe people with freakish immune systems. And those people would have to get back to basics—getting food in their stomachs, having a warm dry place to sleep. Almost all their time and effort would be devoted to activities like that. There wouldn't be any place for all the bullshit that comes with progress and leisure time. No worrying about fulfilling your purpose or having a satisfying life. Your only activity would be staying fucking alive. No one would obsess about getting their life right. There'd be no existential angst. No searching for meaning in life or inner peace. And most of all, for me, there'd be no pursuit of being interested, no quest for kicks, no trying to escape boredom.

"Life would all be boring—morning, noon and night. Nobody would try to nourish their spirit. Talk therapy wouldn't even be a thought in people's minds. Man would be reduced to the basic animal he is, and it would probably be decades, if not centuries, before he rediscovered his soul.

"Everything would be a lot fucking simpler. And it'd be a fucking relief."

The Siamese cat and her friend didn't show at the Oasis. Jack hung out there by himself for a while, watching the evening strollers. Then he went to cruise the bars and found the Siamese cat holding court at Caprice, an upscale lounge for the rich and wanna-bes. Not holding court in the sense of doing all the talking—in fact, she was barely saying anything. She was perched on a leather barstool with padded back and arms, surrounded by male courtiers vying for her attention. Her dark-haired Danish friend sat next to her smoking a Marlboro Light, seemingly okay with her companion getting all the attention. While the friend was fairly attractive, the Euro-lads had their sights set on the queen bee.

The Siamese cat sat there with her long legs crossed and her exquisite head held high, emphasizing her perfect jawline. She wore electric blue spike high heels and a white sheath dress that showed off nicely both her lovely tan and pleasing curves. Her makeup was elegantly done, not too much. Her supplicants talked animatedly over one another. She looked supremely disinterested, an expression Jack surmised was one of her specialties, only occasionally giving one of her acolytes a slight smile.

Jack went to the bathroom to enhance his gift of gab, then got a Dewar's with one ice cube and took a seat across the not yet crowded lounge. Sipping his drink, he occasionally looked at her, which was a true pleasure. There was no doubt she was seriously high maintenance, not a quality he'd deal with for more than a night or two. And he suspected she wasn't overly interesting, either, or all that much fun to hang out with. But she was a stunning example of feminine beauty, and he was in the mood to give it a go, despite the poor odds. Every guy's chances with her type were slim. Women like her displayed themselves every minute they were in public, entertaining offers, overt and covert, toying with their admirers, but it was rare that anybody actually got anywhere with them. But he had nothing else on his wide open schedule, and he was in the mood for a bit of the game. And there was always the long shot chance of unexpected success. Always.

He caught her eye and she gave him a smile. He went outside to a nearby shop and bought a cluster of red grapes. Went back into Caprice, walked over to her, politely excused himself to get through her pack of slickster devotees, and with a flourish presented half of the grapes to her and half to her friend. The Siamese beamed with pleasure and popped one in her mouth. This was the way a princess should be treated.

Instead of joining the Euro-lads, he sat down next to her friend and chatted with her. The friend indicated she wasn't bothered by the situation. It turned out she hadn't known the Siamese very long. They had mutual friends and had both been wanting to go to the Greek islands, so they went together. The friend seemed open to breaking away from the Siamese, and Jack briefly considered switching targets, but there was something non-sexual about the Danish woman, and he decided to keep his eyes on the prize.

He spoke to the Siamese a few times but didn't push it. He would have loved to get her away from her fan club, but there was zero chance of that, so he settled in for the long game. The entire group decamped to a nightclub, and he joined them, at least for a while.

At two in the morning, he was sitting on some outdoor stone steps with the Danish friend, who was smoking and finally beginning to show signs of irritation with the friend, who was standing several feet away with three of her suitors. One of them, a dark, handsome Greek boy, was talking to her heatedly in English, but Jack couldn't follow what the issue was; he assumed frustration. His own interest had waned considerably, but in the course of the evening the Siamese had given him just enough attention and encouragement to keep him around. She knew her stuff.

He'd learned she was only twenty, having previously thought she was at least twenty-five. She was from Göteborg and didn't seem to come from privilege. She referred only to her mother, made no mention of her father. Her physical magnificence was clearly her *raison d'etre*, her currency. She was completely wrapped up in it, luxuriated in it. There was of course a strong market for what she had on offer, especially in the Mediterranean summertime hot spots. Jack could tell she'd made a provincial error in choosing Kyros for her Greek island holiday. Next time she'd go to Mykonos for sure. She was still learning how best to capitalize on her value.

At three in the morning, Jack stood in a dark backstreet with the Danish woman, and a few feet away the handsome Greek boy talked angrily to the Siamese, with a friend of his lingering nearby, seemingly for moral support. Jack had gathered that the Greek boy had met the two young women almost as soon as they got off the ferry, and had quickly persuaded them to come stay with him at his family's summer mansion in the most posh part of town. He assured them they would have their own bedroom, and was good on his word. He was immediately and utterly besotted with the Siamese. Jack assumed she epitomized feminine desirability from his Greek rich kid point of view, and he couldn't see beyond that. He paid for everything for both of them wherever they went, and showered the Siamese with gifts, including some pricey jewelry. And had gotten absolutely nowhere with her, according to her friend, but wouldn't give up. Now he was standing in the dark, passionately proclaiming the most profound love for her. It was painful to watch. She oozed indifference, which just seemed to spur him on to new depths of self-abasement. It occurred to Jack that maybe his own chances were looking up, but he doubted it.

At five in the morning, their motley quintet had repaired to an after-hours club. The Greek boy tried a different tack, making a big effort to be upbeat and convivial. He was even being cordial to Jack, though it was clear they were rivals.

At five-thirty, Jack's last scintilla of interest disintegrated, and he walked home tiredly by himself through the dark, empty streets. The night had been a complete washout, though he accepted it with equanimity. He'd gone into it with his eyes open. It struck him, however, that right on the heels of his failure of manhood with Elizabeth possibly hadn't been the best time to embark on an expedition so unlikely to bear fruit.

The shadow people hung back behind him, not intruding. They were beginning to frighten him a little.

––––––––––

"I've whored around a lot," Jack said to Jenkins one evening at the Oasis. Timmy was waiting tables. "I've behaved abominably at times. I've been with women I couldn't even begin to relate to. I've stooped low. Every guy has on occasion, whether they'll admit it or not. I mean, there was one night on a beach in Portugal . . . You wind up in a situation like that and afterward you wish you could just push a button and make 'em disappear. Or make yourself disappear, equally as effective. But there's hardly any of it I'd take back." He shook his head, savoring the memories. "I've had some beyond-intense experiences. And there are few feelings in this world like peak sexual excitement. I mean, at the height of your pleasure when you're just . . . just lost in it, your whole being floating in nothingness, and there's absolutely nothing else even close to your sphere of consciousness. You're 'right here, right now' in the fullest sense of the phrase. That's what I call being truly interested, not one goddamn iota of boredom." He laughed, amused with himself.

"I've had some times with women I never wanted to see again. In fact, I've had more of those than the other kind. But Christ, let me tell you, I've been with women for one night who I'll remember on my death bed—sexual chemistry combined with erotic. . . erotic zeal that doesn't get any more white hot. And to me, that says it was all worth it—self-loathing and all, the absence of real connection, the sad loneliness that comes after. Like the man said, 'Take your pleasure while it lasts.' Truer words were never spoken."

Do you realize how you sound? Jenkins thought of asking him, but didn't bother. He was used to Jack spinning off into thought rambling, and knew that with speed revving his engine, there wasn't much point in trying to make a point.

Strangely enough, he fairly often found Jack interesting to listen to. Not in the sense that what he said was appealing or relatable, but rather in an over-the-top, outlandish way. It was like being tuned in directly to a tortured madness that every so often made some kind of bizarre sense. Jack's life had been so different from Jenkins' that Jenkins couldn't really imagine it. It was completely alien to him.

Jenkins had spent most of his life having only low-grade diversions. He hadn't interacted with a lot of people who had much to say beyond the ordinary everyday bullshit, very few with any variety of conversational topics, and none with the special damage that the world of privilege can inflict. He'd mostly interacted with the underbelly of society, lowlifes and folks who'd been dealt a tough hand. He didn't expect people to have much of interest to say. Jack was a distinct change, even if an extremely unbalanced one.

It struck Jenkins that Jack had obviously thought hard about a lot of what he said, and believed it. He had formed his own world-view. Jenkins wasn't sure he had a world-view of his own, and suspected most people he'd crossed paths with didn't either. He'd never delved very deeply into trying to understand life. For the most part, it hadn't occurred to him to try. He didn't come close to buying into Jack's warped scheme of things, but still it was something to listen to.

"Another thing," said Jack. "When you get over on a top-quality woman, a beautiful, elegant woman who's smart and got a lot of other things going on—you're there talking to her, giving it your all, and you feel her responding positively to you—there's no rush like it in the world. At that moment, you are the motherfucking man. Filled to the brim with euphoria. And in a moment like that, boredom is just a vague philosophical concept, not remotely a concern. Doesn't exist. You're completely in the moment, engaged to the hilt."

Jack had one more glimpse of the Siamese. A few evenings after the washout with her, he was walking by the Oasis to see if anybody was there he wanted to talk to, and there she was—on the open rear deck of a sleek motor yacht docked with its back to the wharf, in the midst of a glamorous cocktail party. The yacht had a prime location at the mid-point of the promenade. The party was in full swing, with uniformed crew members serving drinks and hors d'oeuvres. The revelers consisted of a half-dozen young women of the same ilk as the Siamese; her friend wasn't there. There were two older men, sixty-five at least, whose manner suggested they were the hosts. One of them had a thick head of wavy white hair, dark leathery skin, white trousers, and a sky-blue button-down shirt of fine linen, untucked. And a cravat. He had one arm around the Siamese's waist. The other seeming host had a similar appearance but was smooth and shiny on top, completely bald, and had large jowls hanging down. The soiree was filled out with two handsome, flamboyant young men and a trio of middle-aged women dressed in the clothes of a daring twenty-year-old—they looked like young women who'd hung around far too long. The group convincingly projected a fabulous occasion. They shimmered with awareness of the people strolling by looking their way. Jack couldn't help but feel that their primary goal was to bathe in envy, which struck him as a peculiar objective. *People are all so weird*, he thought. *Each and every one of us. More than any of us are willing to admit, even to ourselves.*

She's found her perfect milieu, he thought, smiling inwardly. He felt no ill will. She was what she was, and there was certainly a place in the world for people like her, a healthy number of places primed and waiting. *I'd love to be a fly on the wall when she discovers St. Tropez. She's going to think she's died and gone to heaven.* He laughed out loud.

CHAPTER 9

Jack was crawling like a slug on the forest floor, making frustratingly slow progress. He was astounded and horrified to realize he had no skin. He was just a blob of bloody flesh and bones dragging himself along. Looking back, he saw his sack of lifeless skin crumpled on the bed of pine needles. He had no idea where he was struggling to get to. All he knew was he was trying to get away from his epidermis, which had been making him squirm in agonizing discomfort, and he'd felt he had to shed it and slither away. He knew none of this made any sense.

Suddenly, he was back inside his skin vomiting, and Jenkins was at his ear whispering severely, "Don't make a fucking sound."

* * *

Jack's meth intake took a sharp increase, turning him into even more of a nocturnal creature. Jenkins and Timmy rarely saw him awake. He was getting concerned about running out, which would happen in a month or so, depending on how fast the powder went up his nose. He didn't feel up to another replenishment trip, though, in theory, he could brutalize himself into one. His ability to endure the rough patches wasn't as brawny as it used to be. An unfamiliar fragility had become part of him. And the claws of his addiction were digging deeper, into the very core of his shredded soul. He knew that cold turkey withdrawal, one where he was still in Greece with no access to his holy drug, would involve body-hugging spasms of torment. He would discover suffering on a whole new level. He got queasy just thinking about it.

For a long time, he'd managed the lure of methamphetamine with a certain iron discipline, for which he took not a small amount of pride. First, he forced himself to take occasional breaks from his use for two weeks or more, sometimes just substantial reductions. And much more importantly, he only snorted. He didn't smoke or inject, which would have given him a more intense, short-lived high, and would have quickly turned him into a slobbering, hard-core junkie. Not that he wasn't a junkie, but there were addicts and there were addicts. Had he smoked crank or used needles, it wouldn't have been possible to travel the world. He'd have been a bigger wreck than he already was, and would have had to base himself somewhere he could always be absolutely certain he could get more. He might have become a street person despite his trust fund, not wanting to waste money on rent or fleabag hotels when it could be used for his habit. He had somehow clung to these self-imposed constraints, which kept him from going down an even more gruesome road. The traveling helped him maintain his resolve.

But he was more anguished than he'd ever been, and was rightly getting scared.

Another morning. With all that entailed. He felt abysmal again. Like a homeless alky waking up facedown on the pavement in a garbage-strewn alley, a gritty imprint on the side of his face, a metaphor that hadn't always been just a metaphor for Jack. Lying in his narrow bed, his person felt like a smashed machine, totaled beyond repair. It struck him that whenever he thought he'd reached rock bottom, he always managed to find some scummy rock and turn it over to find someplace lower, crawling with bugs and worms. He felt bruised, broken, empty. He hurt everywhere, could barely move. He was sick of this. It was getting really tedious.

It was half past one in the afternoon before he emerged into the daylight. He made it down to the harbor front, grabbed a copy of the *Trib* from the rack, and paid for it. Sat down at the café furthest from the Oasis, taking a table in the back row as far under the awning as possible, the only customer there, Ordered coffee and water. Sometimes he just couldn't face the Oasis; there were always people there he was at least acquainted with and had to acknowledge. And worse, the popular café had in some way begun to rub his face in his decomposing life. So sometimes he gave in to the pretense that sitting in a dead café down the row would make a difference.

The *Trib* had a headline saying the temperatures in the eastern Mediterranean were record setting. It had been over a hundred the past few days, and the unrelenting heat was taking a definite toll on him, on top of all the other punishment he was absorbing. He looked around and saw the harbor front was nearly deserted, barely a person in sight, even at the Oasis. The beaches must be packed. Timmy was probably at Banana. In the past week, the sea had been so warm it hadn't even been refreshing to dive into. Jenkins was out with the old fisherman, doing whatever the hell it was he did. The stillness of the town was beyond oppressive.

His broken sunglasses supplemented the shade from the awning in lessening the brutal effect of the sun but reinforced his semi-comatose state as well. It was an effort just to breathe. A layer of sweat that seemed to never dry covered him, keeping his T-shirt and shorts constantly moist.

"Fuck," he said out loud, no one around to hear him. He took out his flask and poured some whiskey in his coffee.

The speed was destroying him. His teeth and gums hurt all the time. When he dared look in a mirror, he saw someone ten years older. His handsome face looked ravaged. He was thin beyond attractiveness, on the verge of emaciation. His nose often leaked blood, and when it didn't, it was stuffed up with mucus and dried blood.

He was running out of steam. And spirit and fortitude. And he still had no idea what he was going to do when he ran out of meth. He'd tried to think of a way to scam a doctor in Athens but hadn't been able to come up with a story that had a chance of holding water. He'd thought about trying a bribe, a practice he knew was well ingrained in modern Greece, but such an approach was risky where drugs were involved. He wondered if they even had meth labs in this country that wasn't looking so wonderful anymore.

I don't want to think about it, his brain snapped at him. Which of course was how he dealt with all his problems. A dark cloud settled into his head. He was experiencing something beyond depression. His spirit seemed to be giving up, surrendering. His despair had definitely lost all remnants of stylishness. His self-loathing had reached new depths, and he was less okay with it. His desperation wasn't quiet anymore at all. It howled with a fury that gave him the feral fears, the feeling that terrified him more than any other.

He saw that the ghost people were sitting silently at various tables around the café. He noticed for the first time that while their long robes were gray, they were somehow translucent at the same time. He had a flash of firing a machine gun. Felt it buck in his hands, saw it spray a zigzag pattern of holes in a whitewashed stone wall, like the bullet holes in Parisian buildings left unrepaired from World War II to remind people of the evil man is capable of.

It seemed like he was going to have to go back to New York, though he couldn't see exactly why since there were no solutions there. It just seemed like that's where he should be if he was going to truly crash and burn. Though he supposed he could do that just about anywhere. He'd certainly seen a fair number of expats crumble into bits in their adopted purgatories, especially in Southeast Asia.

He'd spent a considerable amount of time and effort trying to develop a stimulating, interesting life, thought he'd had a leg up on most people because of his luck in being modestly financially independent, but all he'd accomplished was emptiness and decay. And worst of all, his life was boring, deadeningly boring, the exact thing he'd set out to escape. He was an idiot. A loser. He looked down on all the people who led conventional lives, thought he was better. But he was wrong. You can't build a life out of nothingness. Could it possibly be that discipline, routine, and drudgery were things you had to put up with to construct a meaningful life, providing you with at least a modicum of real satisfaction? Was a modicum of satisfaction all you could hope for? None of these thoughts mattered. He wasn't capable of such an approach at this point anyway. He didn't have a fresh start in him.

What was going to become of him? The question reared its ugly head, as it did so often. He truly had no idea of the answer but knew he was going to find out soon enough.

He glanced through the *Trib*. *Wow. My lucky day—a human interest story. Could be interesting.* An eleven-year-old boy living in an orphanage in Hawaii had gotten into surfing and become very gung ho. Hung out at the surfing beaches all the time, soaking up skills and the culture. He heard the older surfers talking about famous places around the world to surf, great breaks, places like legendary Bondi Beach in Sydney. So one day, he went to the Honolulu airport and figured out which gate was going to be used by a Qantas flight arriving from and returning to Sydney. He hung around the arrival area waiting for the flight. As the arriving passengers walked out into the terminal, he told a stewardess he'd left his jacket on the plane and she let him back on. He hid in one of the bathrooms and flew to Sydney, then got through passport control by saying he'd come to the airport with his mother to meet his uncle and had somehow wandered into the wrong area. He hitchhiked to Bondi and spent the day surfing on borrowed boards. *Must've had plenty of charm*, thought Jack, surfers being on the less friendly end of the social spectrum. The kid only got caught when he tried to pull a runner on the taxi driver who drove him back to the airport.

Jack put the newspaper down and sat there staring out at the south-facing harbor, which his guidebook said was one of the prettiest in the

Aegean. There were two uninhabited islands in the distance that gave the scene a pleasing balance. His brain stewed with thoughts and feelings.

A sensation gradually welled up inside him and came into focus as a feeling of realizing some fundamental truth about life, some profound insight. But as he tried to find the words to express it, it slipped away. Crumbled into mental dust.

He returned to the apartment to lie down for a while.

Early that evening, he woke up from a deep, leaden sleep, drenched in sweat. He dragged himself to the bathroom and filled the tub from the tap labeled cold. Took the two full ice cube trays from the freezer compartment in the fridge and dropped them whole in the water. Laid down in the tub until the water lost its coolness, which took all of about five minutes. Stepping limply out, he felt slightly revived.

Outside, the sun had dropped behind the pine-covered hills, and the heat had let up a bit. He walked through the village; all the clean bright white grated on him. His habit of imagining shooting a pistol occurred reflexively. The shadow people trailed behind. Or were they ghost people, he couldn't keep it straight. The two tall ones picked up their pace, or maybe it was a glide, so they were right behind him, one at either shoulder, and the shorter ones scurried or skimmed along behind.

At the Oasis, he was keenly relieved to find Timmy and Jenkins. Timmy wasn't working and to his surprise was sitting with Jenkins. The two had developed some sort of rapport, which Jack was actually glad for. It was helping keep them a threesome, which he wasn't ready to give up just yet, though he was contributing next to nothing.

"Hey there," he said, sitting down.

Jenkins leaned his chair back on two legs and looked at him. "Man, you look like shit. You did yourself some damage last night."

Jack had little memory of the previous night and wondered what in particular Jenkins was referring to. How big an idiot had he made of himself? "Yeah, well, these things happen," he said. "Maybe tonight I'll achieve total anesthesia."

Neither Jenkins nor Timmy reacted. He thought he saw some surprise on their faces at his wasted appearance but figured he was being paranoid.

"How's the fishing?" he asked.

"Not bad. Good catch today. Stavros was happy." Jenkins sipped his Carlsberg. Timmy lit a cigarette.

"I was just saying," Jenkins went on, "the people here, they ain't got it half bad. They're poor, but it's an okay place to be poor. It's a helluva lot better than living in a shack in Appalachia working in a coal mine, or living on skid row in some big city. I can never understand homeless people who live in cities, especially cold weather cities. If I was poor, this is the kind of place I'd come to. Lead a simple life. Good weather, good food, things don't cost much. Gradually become a part of the community, as much as an outsider can. The way I see it, if you don't have a lot going for yourself, you lower your expectations and find a life on a scale you can manage. Make it work for you."

Jack felt his ugliness well up inside him. "Yeah. And in the off-season, you turn into a hard-core alcoholic. Or maybe even not wait for the off-season. After the tourists are gone, you go stir crazy from the isolation and absolutely nothing going on for months on end. These island paradises always seem so great in the high season, when they're all vibrant and pumping. But they can be god-awful miserable when there's only the villagers left and the businesses are closed or empty, and there's zero to do.

"But hey," his tone became blatantly sarcastic, "maybe the two of you should settle down here and open a bar. Lead the sweet simple life."

Timmy got up and went inside the café.

"That's what I like about you, Jack. You really know how to give a lift to a social occasion."

Jack shrugged. "Heartattack and Vine" was playing on the café's outdoor speakers. They regularly played the album there from beginning to end, and it always sounded great, despite the frequency. Jack thought it was great they played albums like that in entirety. Back in the States, he didn't know of a bar that did the same. Jenkins hummed along for a few bars of "On the Nickel," as the troubadour's raspy voice wafted through the evening air: "What becomes of all the little boys? Who run away from home. The world just keeps getting bigger. Once you get out on your own."

"Christ," said Jack, "I didn't know you were maudlin."

Jenkins didn't know what the word meant. He'd look it up later.

A swarthy young woman walked by strutting her stuff, provocatively dressed—tube top, stretchy miniskirt, teetering in white high heels on the uneven pavement.

More nastiness rose up inside Jack. "You know, there ain't nothing worse than a skank who won't put out. I mean, what other point do they got?"

"Jack, shut the fuck up."

He did. For a minute or so. Then in a distant voice said, "I was outside a club once in the East Village, slam-dancing place on Avenue A, and I see this guy come out wearing a T-shirt that says on the front 'Fuck 'em and kill 'em.'" He took out his flask and had a swig. "Bold sentiment to wear on your chest, don't you think?"

"Listen, Jack. I'm not in the mood for your bullshit tonight. So just shut the fuck up." Jenkins lit a Marlboro and took a deep drag. "And as far as I can tell, I'm one of the last people on Earth willing to put up with you, so I strongly urge you to not push it."

Jack ordered a beer from a passing waitress.

"What the hell you got against women, Jack? There's a word for that, right?"

"Misogyny."

"Yeah, so . . . ?"

"Oh, I don't know. Women are okay. I guess I just like to blame everybody else for being stuck being me." He pulled at the scraggly growth on his chin. "I don't see women the way I see guys. From guys, at least you have the possibility of having some interesting conversation—a meeting of the minds once in a while, conversation that's somewhat linear and rational, talking with someone who occasionally understands what you mean. There are only two good things you get from women—sex and ego-food. I know that's an asinine thing to say. Intellectually, I get that women deserve to be treated equal with guys, but I don't get the same things from them I get from guys. Not that I get such so much from guys, either. I don't get much from anybody. And that's on me, I know. I'm like a failed nation where the government falls apart and the society descends into chaos. I'm a failed person. I have a failed life. Hey, it happens. *C'est la vie.*" He took another slug from his flask, despite the beer sitting in front of him.

"But what the hell, why stop there?" He perked up. "If I'm going to offend, I might as well offend with authority. So, I'll throw out the flipside of the two good things you get from women: the two negatives— rejection and disappointment. Rejection, that one's obvious, and I'm okay with it. Like I always say," he grinned crookedly, "if you ain't getting rejected, you ain't trying hard enough. You're not getting the best women you can. I accept rejection as part of the game. Got no problem with it. But disappointment, that's more complicated. Women who don't reject you, who go for you, maybe even fall for you, they always come up short in terms of providing you with the companionship and conversation you want. And that's why sooner or later you want to go hang out with a guy. So you can talk about the stuff you want to talk about and have a chance of being understood."

He lapsed into silence.

"So maybe I do hate women," he picked up. "And that's one more way I'm a despicable person. I've spent so much time and energy cultivating my repulsive persona, there's no undoing it. It's who I am, who I'm always going to be."

He went silent again, withdrew into himself. Jenkins sipped his beer. "The other night I was at the Kentavros." Jack couldn't quite manage to stop talking, and continued in a faraway voice. "It was late. The place was getting ready to close. And there was this woman, decent looking, giving me come-on looks from across the bar. And my knee-jerk reaction was the usual—go for it. But then I thought, I'll have to talk to her. And maybe go someplace else for a drink. And talk some more. And listen to her tell me about herself. And tell her some things about me, even if I make it up. And maybe then I'll bed her. Or maybe not. And I thought to myself, all I want to do is fuck her. I don't want to talk to her or get to know her, or tell her about myself or any of that shit. I just want to fuck her. And I don't even want to do that all that much.

"Most guys at one time or another have thought about walking up to a hot-looking woman somewhere who they don't know, and simply asking, 'Do you want to fuck?' Just like that. They've *thought* about it but never done it, or even come close. Because they know it wouldn't get 'em anywhere. I mean, there might be some one-in-a-million head-cases out there who'd go for it. You hear stories. But with virtually all women, an approach like that will get you either a slap or a drink thrown in your face. And rightly so, I guess. 'Cause women want you to talk to them. They want you to get to know one another.

"So, I'm sitting there at the Kentravos looking at this woman across the bar, and I realize that's the fucking problem. Women want you to talk to them. They want to be treated like people."

———————————

Later that evening, after the evening gave way to the night, the three of them still sat at the Oasis, each mildly drunk in their own way. The bad atmosphere from Jack's earlier nastiness had dissipated.

"So, Roy," Timmy said—she'd taken to calling him by his first name—"when are you going to bring us some fish?"

Jenkins looked at her questioningly.

"You go out," she said, "catch all these fish, and you never bring any home."

"What are we gonna do with a fish? Who's gonna clean it? Cook it? And what, the three of us are going to sit down together and have a home-cooked meal? Doesn't sound like us."

"Why not? You bring me a nice, fresh fish and I'll clean it and cook it. And I'll guarantee you it'll taste good. I know what I'm doing. Just ask Stavros for a really good fish. He'll know which one. You've done all this work for him, for free retsina, which you don't even like. He owes you a good fish. Come on." Her manner was friendly but insistent.

"He's offered."

"Well, then, it's settled," Jack chimed in, exaggeratedly upbeat. "To-morrow night. Jenkins, you get the fish. Timmy, you tell me the other stuff you'll need to fix a proper dinner and I'll get all that. Okay?"

Timmy and Jenkins looked at one another dubiously.

"Jenksy," boomed a deep English voice from across the esplanade. "You bloody bugger. There you are."

The light of a streetlamp showed a large man with a red face in white trousers, white belt, white loafers, and a lime-green polo shirt bulging at the stomach. He strode over to them with a woman in tow—frosted blonde hair, deep tan, wrinkled face, white tennis skirt and sneakers, pink top.

"Bloody 'ell, Jenksy. You're an 'ard man to find. I been looking for you 'igh and low." Sandy hair, face puffy, looked to be in his mid-fifties.

"Rafe." Jenkins nodded at him. "I'm right here in plain sight."

"But 'ell, man, you weren't where you were s'posed to be. You were s'posed to be in Affens, my man." His tone had taken on an edge and his manner conveyed he was used to the edge being heeded.

"You were late," Jenkins said evenly. "I left word where I'd be. Otherwise, you wouldn't be standing here right now, growling like a bear."

Rafe didn't react for a few moments, then laughed uproariously. "Jenksy, that's what I like 'bout you. Never get rattled. Good man. Now, introduce me to your mates. Looks like you're moving in some new circles."

Introductions were made. As Rafe looked Jack over, Jack felt as if his addiction and shattered self were glowing bright red.

The woman's name was Deedee. Rafe grabbed a fifth chair from the next table and the couple sat down with them.

"So, what has Jenksy told you 'bout 'imself?"

"Rafe," Jenkins said firmly. "You found me. Nothing's changed."

"Oh, don't worry. Your secrets are safe with me." Rafe laughed raucously. He turned to Jack and Timmy. "I can assure you good people that this lad enjoys his work. Positively delights innit. And that ain't the 'alf of it. You should see him in action."

Jack had never stopped having a clear picture in his mind's eye of the American's face shattering the full shot glass on the bar, with Jenkins' meaty hand on the back of his head.

"So, Rafe," Jenkins said, "how're you enjoying the Greek islands? You came in the cruiser?"

"Too many bubbles for me. Can't stand 'em. Peasants. Prefer the other end of the Med. More sophisticated, know what I mean? And the food's better by far. The calamari here is crap, and I love my calamari. The wine's undrinkable. Tastes like bloody turpentine." He glared at a table of tourists who were looking over and listening. They turned away quickly.

"Yeah, we rode up in the motor yacht," he went on. "Sammy's along too. With Cynthia. We're docked in the marina just 'round the point. Why don't you bring your friends 'round and we'll 'ave ourselves a proper drinks do? Aperitifs and whores-devores. Classy like. You know me."

"I'll come with you," Jenkins said. "We can talk." He stood up, mussing his mustache.

"Oo, that's a shame. It's a lovely vessel," Rafe said to Jack and Timmy. "And Jenksy, your lady friend is a stunner."

Jenkins looked at him steadily, evenly, not saying anything.

"Lovely to meet you both," Rafe said with exaggerated politeness. "Hope to see you again soon." Deedee hadn't said a word since "Hello."

CHAPTER 10

Jack put the silly red wig onto his head and the Zorro mask on. An observer suddenly materialized several feet in the air above them, hovering. Jack knew the onlooker was a product of his unhinged mind, was a variation of his self. As if his spirit had left his body and floated upward, and was now looking down on them. A witness to the proceedings, as seemed appropriate.

* * *

"Ain't life grand," Jack exclaimed, sitting on the balcony with Jenkins and raising a glass of Chianti to the night sky. He wasn't in a bad mood, but still he felt the urge to be caustic and sarcastic, which could easily lead to ugliness. Thunderclouds had moved in and out of his head all day.

Timmy was in the kitchen area preparing their fish dinner. She worked with assurance and clearly knew what she was doing.

Whenever Jack glanced in through the open balcony doors, he saw the shadow people standing around the main room against the walls at random intervals, with a tall one and a short one sitting on opposite ends of the couch, all watching him. They made no sound directly, but their presence, which Jack was making a mighty effort to ignore, seemed to somehow trigger screeches and cries that reverberated outside in the distance, fading in and out as the wind gusted.

Jack was feeling agitated, on the verge of hysteria. He wasn't sure he was going to be able to hold it together through the meal. He felt as if he might crack into three or four large pieces. Then what would he do?

"So," he said to Jenkins, trying to sound casual, "you say you're doing some transport work for your friend Rafe? He's a scoundrel, the real deal. I don't think he liked me."

"He probably thought you were a degenerate."

"Come on, Jenkins, you got to tell me. What do you really do with those shady characters? They're not above board. Rafe's a reprobate if I ever saw one."

Another word to look up, thought Jenkins. Jack's fancy word choices were getting downright annoying. "I told you," he responded, "it's none of your goddamn business. And I'm cutting you a lot of slack 'cause of our dinner tonight. So back the fuck off. Now."

Stavros had selected a large, nice-looking fish for them. He'd said the English name was sea bream and that he didn't catch them very often, at least not this good. He'd presented it to Jenkins with great pride.

Timmy had cleaned it expertly, no sign of squeamishness, and cut it into two large chunks, which were sautéing in two frying pans with olive oil, white wine, and diced garlic and onions. She had a bowl of chopped tomatoes soaking in oil, vinegar, salt and pepper to spread as a blanket of garnish over the fish when it was done. She'd made orso as a side dish, which Jenkins had never had but was willing to try. She was in a good mood, despite the strange dynamics of their trio. She wasn't sure how she'd wound up with these two particular misfits. The people she clicked with were usually offbeat, sometimes with good results, sometimes bad. With Jack, the result clearly had not been good, but there was still a residue of positive feeling, enough for the evening, or so she thought. With Jenkins, the jury was still out. In any event, she was feeling some normalcy for the first time in months, and she liked it. Being out of her comfort zone for an extended period had been good for her in any number of ways, but doing something ordinary and familiar felt good as well.

Jack had bought some taramasalata and a fresh baguette, and the three of them were already smearing the pink paste on torn pieces of bread, wolfing them down. Another culinary first for Jenkins. He was surprised to find he liked it.

The occasion was the most alien for Jenkins. For most of his adult life, he'd eaten meals alone or with coworkers, and more for sustenance than pleasure or socializing. He could count on both hands the number of times in his adult life he'd sat down to a home-cooked meal with companions. He'd felt ill at ease at the beginning of the evening, but managed to get comfortable enough to enjoy himself. Contact with people had always been awkward for him to one degree or another.

They sat down at their small round Formica table, and Jenkins raised his glass. "Salud."

"Cheers," Timmy chimed in.

"Ya mas," said Jack. "May the wind at your back always be your own."

J. J. Cale's "Cocaine" was playing on the cheap boom box Jack had bought when they first moved in, and he sang along: "If you want to ride on and your spirit is gone, cocaine."

"Is that why you do it?" asked Jenkins in a conversational tone.

"I don't do it," Jack said. "Cocaine is bullshit. It makes you feel like superman for twenty minutes, and then you're chasing the feeling all night long. But speed," he said with exaggerated reverence. "Speed makes you feel like God for hours."

Jenkins and Timmy thought about this, each in their own way imagining Jack's experience. They both knew that whatever deity-like episodes he had, they were interspersed with crippling despair. They each saw Jack as one of the most isolated people they'd ever known. Jenkins was isolated too, but in a different way. He was self-sufficient and at ease with long periods of solitude. Comfortable in his own skin. Jack's detachment was glaringly unhealthy. Even so, it wasn't a complete coincidence the two men had become companions. Two orphans, each a casualty of life in his own way, encountering one another in the casual social atmosphere of the Greek islands.

The fantastic aromas of the food had them all salivating, and when Timmy put the plates on the table, with the food arranged in a visually appealing way, they gobbled it down—even Jack, who'd laid off the speed so as to have an appetite. The sea bream was succulent, full of fantastic flavors, the ideal texture. The orso was *al dente* and comple- mented the fish perfectly. Timmy had concocted a tasty dressing for the salad. Effusive compliments were lavished on the chef, and she glowed with pleasure. For dessert, they had Neapolitan ice cream, with coffee. The meal was over quickly, consumed in a fraction of the time it took to prepare.

They all cleaned up, including Jack. As Timmy was putting away the last few things, Jack and Jenkins moved their chairs back out onto the balcony, sat and put their feet up on the railing, looked out at the night. Jack took out his flask, which shone dully in the dark, and had a long drink. Offered it perfunctorily to Jenkins, but he already had an open beer.

"Okay, Jenkins, I get it." Jack tried to sound casual. "You aren't going to tell me about your nefarious activities, but before your shady friends left, I heard Rafe talking to you about something high level going on. Something around here."

Jenkins stiffened. "What the hell are you talking about?"

"Oh, come on, don't lose your rag with me. You know what I'm like. I couldn't help myself." Jack felt his attempt at nonchalance slipping badly.

Jenkins scowled at him with menace. Jack plunged ahead, aware of the risk but under sway of a compulsion he couldn't resist. "I followed you guys when you went back to their boat. I walked out on the dock like I belonged there and stood next to Rafe's boat. Listened in as best I could, on and off. Had to walk away a couple of times when people came along. And you guys were below deck, so I couldn't hear all of what you were saying. But I was lucky—a couple of the portholes were open."

"You puny little shit. Wha'dja hear? Give it to me plain and simple. No bullshit. Tell me what you heard."

Jack sensed Jenkins transforming in front of him into someone fully capable of serious violence. He flashed back to his first impression. And the barbaric explosion in the bar. He felt a real physical threat coming his way from Jenkins for the first time. He realized that at the Kentavros, when he'd pressed him about being a mercenary, Jenkins had still been in control, hadn't been angry to the point of the primal savagery in him emerging.

Jack felt he had no choice but to go on. "I heard you're supposed to provide them with, you know, like you said, some maritime transport services. It sounded well-paid, and you don't need to know what the cargo is."

Jenkins stood and loomed over Jack, aggressively invading his space. Jack tried but couldn't bring himself to look up at him. It occurred to him that Jenkins might throw him off the balcony. He wondered what injuries that would inflict. Depended on how he landed, he supposed.

"And?"

"I heard about some other job, something about a VIP staying in a villa on an island near here. I couldn't hear who it was. But I could tell it was confidential, something people aren't supposed to know about."

"You—stupid—fucking—idiot. Do yourself an enormous favor and forget everything you heard."

"The weird thing was," Jack went on in a shaky voice, "I couldn't tell whether the job was working for the guy, or just the opposite—killing him. Rafe seemed to be talking about one thing, but then it sounded like the other. It was hard to follow."

"Jesus Christ, you stupid shit. It's a goddamn good thing Rafe is gone. You wouldn't want to find out what he'd do if he knew you'd listened in on him. He's a hard man. Don't like loose ends. Deals with problems fast and final. Don't take chances."

Jack sat very still.

What's this mean? Jenkins thought quickly. *The little shit doesn't really know much, not if he's telling the truth. But I should minimize the risk, as always. What is the risk? Something happens and the leak gets traced back to me. Unlikely, but who needs it? I don't like it. Goddamn it. I shoulda stayed put in Athens. Shit.*

But he didn't hear enough. And he's useless, couldn't do anything if he tried. Still, I wish to fuck he hadn't heard anything. He's unstable, unreliable. A disaster waiting to happen. Most dangerous to himself, but a guy like him can easily do damage to the people around him. He's not exactly careful in the way he runs his life.

Jack wondered what was coming, whether he'd really gone too far. Jenkins would probably focus on practical considerations, wouldn't get worked up about things like respecting privacy or etiquette, crap like that. But Jack had no idea what the practical considerations were in this situation.

"You fucking worm," Jenkins said. "If this ever comes back on me, in any way, I will fucking bury you."

Jack believed him. Maybe more than he'd ever believed anybody about anything. The worst of the storm seemed to have passed, but he still didn't feel he was in the clear. "Hey, man, I don't know anything. I don't know who the guy is, where he is, or even what the job is."

"People like you blab. It's how you're made. You tell all kinds of crap to strangers in bars all the time, anything that comes into that mess you call a brain. I pick up one whisper of this, and you're gonna wish you weren't you. I'm dead serious. And I will hear about it, believe me. It's a small village. So keep your fucking trap shut."

Timmy came out with a glass of wine, joining them on the balcony. She immediately sensed the tension crackling in the air and wondered what could have happened in such a short time to change the vibe so dramatically, but didn't ask. The three of them drank in silence. Jenkins and Timmy smoked cigarettes. The camaraderie conjured up by their dinner was gone, erased.

Jack went into the bathroom and did way too big a blast, felt his heart hammer in his chest. He got the acrid taste of the drug in the back of his throat, which he hated. He went to the kitchen area and drank from a bottle of cheap whiskey to wash it away. Took a glass from the cabinet and filled it with the harsh liquor, without ice, then drank some more. He had a flash of spraying the room with a machine gun, riddling all the goddamn ghost people with bullets so they'd stop watching him from the darkness inside their gnome-like hoods.

Back when he'd first noticed the shadow people, he'd thought he was too rational to ever take them seriously. They were optical illusions brought on by his long-term meth use. They couldn't be more than that. But at this point, he had no sane explanation for the progress they'd made. They appeared with regularity now, and not in a fleeting way anymore—they hung around—and they manifested an increasing variety of behavior. This was all forcing him to consider the possibility that he was going mad. *Wouldn't that be something?* They showed up every day now at one time or another. And he was getting used to them, which couldn't be good. What if he started talking to them, which he'd felt the urge to do a few times?

He went back out on the balcony and sat back down. He felt his ugliness rise up inside him like vomit reaching the back of his throat. "Hey, Jenkins. You know why God gave women pussies?"

Jenkins and Timmy exchanged looks.

"To keep men from putting a bounty on them." Jack gave a harsh bark of laughter.

Undeterred by the lack of response, or more likely goaded by it, he went on, "You ever hear the one about when God first created Adam and Eve?"

"Give it a rest, Jack," Jenkins said quietly, a clear signal.

Jack recognized the danger sign, but his intrinsic self-destructiveness drove him on. "No, no. You got to hear this one. It's great. You see, God originally forgot to give Adam and Eve sex organs. One of his angels comes up from the Garden of Eden and points out the oversight to him. God says, 'Okay, well, listen, go over to the workshop and fix up some genitalia for them. And then go down and install them so we can get the whole procreation thing going. But stop by my office on your way out, and show me what you come up with.' So the angel went to the workshop and made some genitalia, and stopped by God's office. God takes a quick look and says, 'Yeah, those are fine. Great. Go ahead.' As the angel turns to go, though, God says, 'Oh and by the way, don't forget to give the cunt to the dumb one.'" Jack cackled like a lunatic, well beyond whatever laughter was justified by the joke. He couldn't stop. Got himself somewhat under control, but kept giggling and snickering on and off for a couple of minutes.

While Jack was getting such a big kick out of himself, Jenkins decided he was going to hit him in the face. Hard. See what effect that had on his laughter. But he moved deliberately rather than with the instantaneous speed he knew was the right way to dispense violence, and Timmy had an opportunity to burst out, "Christ, Jack. You are such a complete asshole. It's not just an act you put on, like you try to pretend. You really are an ugly person inside."

"That's funny. That's exactly what my dear old mother said to me when I was twelve, shortly before she passed. She looked at me across the dining room table one evening and said, 'Jack Ferris, you are an ugly person inside.' I'm sure she'd be glad to know I've lived up to her early assessment. Shame my parents never got to see my repugnance in its full splendor."

He'd seen Jenkins ready himself for action and quickly kept talking to forestall whatever was coming. "You know, I never even felt bad about getting them killed. Who the hell were they to me anyway? I only saw them a grand total of about a month a year. And they weren't exactly brimming with affection for their bad seed. They found institutions to deal with me, form me. They were oblivious to the cruelty and sadism woven into the fabric of those places. Or maybe they weren't.

"These places are the same malignant institutions that produce the patrician thugs who run the US. And we wonder why the people who govern us never, ever approach a single decision by asking the question: what's the right thing to do? Never.

"I was brought up immersed in malevolence," he finished lamely.

"Oh, poor little Jackie," Timmy spat out. "Let's all feel sorry for Jackie boy—the self-pity champion of the world. They don't come any whinier than you.

"You couldn't have a healthy relationship with a woman if your life depended on it. You have big gaping holes in you where there's supposed to be the stuff that makes people human. You've never just had sex with a woman. You've always fucked them. You've definitely never even come close to making love. You don't even know what that means." She gulped for air.

"The way you see things, fucking a woman is doing something bad to her. In your twisted mind, they're degrading themselves by letting you fuck them. And that's exactly what you want—to degrade them. Big-time womanizer, Jack the world traveler, seducing women all over the globe, getting 'em to spread their legs and let him in.

"'*Getting over on 'em.*' I couldn't believe it the first time I heard you say that. What the fuck do you think you're getting over on 'em? Fooling them into thinking they're having real contact with a real human being? Tricking them into thinking they're making a genuine connection? You really are the master trickster—fooling all those poor unsuspecting women to . . . to try to achieve some intimacy with a piece of shit. What a joke—intimacy with Jack Ferris, the non-human through and through.

"You're pathetic." She calmed slightly. "A bloody cripple. Yeah, I know, you got a shit deal as a kid, and that's what made you such a total asshole. Which makes you happy. You're the living proof of just how bad you got fucked over. You're the justification of yourself, why you're entitled to be such a complete scumbag.

"But let me tell you something you probably missed. Though, who knows, maybe it'll give you the best goddamn reason yet for your boundless self-pity. Listen: Nobody—Gives—A—Good—Goddamn—About—You—Jackie Boy. Not a single fucking person."

She started to cry, not loudly, but she gave a sob and tears flowed. Telling Jack off hadn't given her much relief. She had an enormous amount of pent-up feelings, built up over the last few months. They'd all gushed out in a flurry of words and now took the form of the salty liquid streaming down her face.

A long silence followed, punctuated by her quiet weeping. Neither Jack nor Jenkins had ever seen Timmy get really worked up about anything before, nothing even close to an outburst like this. She lit a Marlboro and took a couple of deep drags.

"Well," said Jack, with mock lightness, "hard to get happy after that. Think I'll head out to hustle some women." He went inside, grabbed his jean jacket, and left the apartment.

Timmy leaned over the railing, with her elbows resting on it. Jenkins had sat back down. Neither said anything for a while.

"I don't know why I let him get to me like that," she said eventually. "I know what he's like. I've got no illusions about him. I never fell in love with him. Stopped myself as soon as I saw what he was like. I didn't see his nasty side until later. Traveling with him, he was always decent to me, polite. Of course, it didn't take me all that long to pick up on his . . . his troubled soul. But as you know, his trouble is all of his own making, and I'm not convinced he even has a soul." She gave a wry smile that Jenkins could barely see in the dark, but what he could see of it made him think of her spunky resilience and the appeal it imbued her with. Her distress somehow made her look more beautiful than ever.

"His goddamn problems are so much less than most people's," she went on. "He has problems of luxury. He has the freedom to decide what his life is going to be without having to worry how he's gonna pay the bills. He hasn't had to deal with the basic realities that dominate most people's lives. He could have done a million things. It was all there for him. And all he's managed is to become a miserable repulsive person, who does nothing, has nothing. It's really unbelievable." She heaved a sigh.

She'd left out that she was still slightly susceptible to his lanky sexual aura. She still regularly saw women look at him with desire, including a fair number of older well-dressed women, often in the company of obviously affluent spouses. He was unkempt but he definitely had something. Something potent. There was no denying it, as much as she would have liked to.

"Well, he sure fucked up a nice evening," Jenkins said. "We almost had ourselves a good time, like normal people." He wanted to say more, but couldn't think of what.

"I've got to go out for a walk," she said quietly.

Jenkins sat alone in the dark and thought about Jack listening in on Rafe. He knew how Rafe would react if he knew. On general principles alone, of which Rafe had about ten for every situation. He was gone, though. He'd left earlier that day, around noon, roaring out of the marina, looking back and flipping the V-sign—maybe at Jenkins standing on the pier, maybe at the island, maybe bubbles in general. Jenkins had learned in Marbella that bubble was Cockney rhyming slang for a Greek. Bubble and squeak, Greek. The Brits called Jenkins a septic—Yank, septic tank.

Jenkins and Rafe had replaced their loose Athens arrangement with a fixed, detailed plan. On a date thirteen days off, Jenkins was to be at a harbor on the Tunisian coast, arriving via inconspicuous ground transport for the last leg of his travel. A yacht would be waiting there with all the external trappings of an expensive vacation charter, but with numerous custom-rigged compartments below deck. Jenkins would take it across the Mediterranean solo, never advisable but doable in the decent weather that should prevail at this time of year. And deliver its contents to a secluded bay on the Croatian coast identified by flashing red lights on the night he was expected, and if need be each of the next two nights. Rafe hadn't said what the cargo would be, but he only had one product line, and Jenkins knew from listening to the Brits that since Tito's death, centuries-old tensions in the Balkans had been flaring up again, and the well-financed Croats were definitely not going to be caught unprepared when the seemingly inevitable hostilities broke out. Jenkins' hefty cash compensation, which he'd already received a third of, was coming directly from Rafe. He'd have no money dealings with anyone else.

He went inside and got another beer, turned out the lights in the main room, and returned to the balcony. He felt comfortable and relaxed by himself. Solitude was the state he was most used to by far. He'd stopped trying to be at ease with other people a long time ago. He understood on some basic level that everyone was alone, even those who were surrounded by people all the time. He figured he was just facing up to reality, living life the way it was, while almost everyone else was in denial. Thinking like that was a large part of how he coped with being a loner, and with a future that was unknown most of the time. It took a certain type of person to go through life knowing only how things were at the moment and for the next month or two at most. Jenkins was okay with uncertainty. It was all he'd ever known, even in the army, which had its own special brand of unpredictability.

His eyes gradually adjusted to the dark and he could make out the murky landscape in front of him. He thought back to when he'd briefly been a radio operator in the army, before he'd been transferred to supply operations for unspecified reasons. He'd been stationed at Khe Sanh, the heavily fortified combat base surrounded by VC-controlled territory, an island in the midst of enemy territory, which for some reason defying comprehension, the army had felt the need to maintain, despite the French debacle at Dien Bien Phu, a similar installation that had been overrun. The last time he'd worked as a radio operator had been with a captain at the base communicating with a platoon in the bush. Platoons were supposed to be led by captains, but this platoon was led by a lieutenant because there was a shortage of soldiers qualified to be a captain. Jenkins didn't know the lieutenant personally, but from seeing him around the base had a strong sense of him as a very tough soldier, in a place where it was hard to stand out that way. It showed in the deferential way the other soldiers treated him. And Jenkins could almost see the gray-blue aura hanging in the air around him, the one that showed you were hard, able to rule your fear.

The captain had received orders to have the platoon take a particular hilltop. The orders came from a general on a battleship lying out in the South China Sea, who'd visited Khe Sanh maybe once or twice and had definitely never been in the bush. *He's not even on the mainland*, thought Jenkins. *He's sitting on a goddamn ship, outside artillery range.*

The hilltop was in the middle of nowhere. There was nothing there other than a couple of squads of NVA, maybe more, thoroughly dug in at the top. There was no sensible reason to do battle to gain possession of the position. Jenkins studied the topographical maps and could see it was at least ten clicks from any villages or land cleared for farming. There was no indication that anybody had ever wanted it or used it for anything, even before the war. The hill rose steeply and was almost all rock, with hardly any foliage. It would be extraordinarily hard to take, maybe impossible by foot soldiers alone. But the general sitting on the ship had decided it had to be taken, and taken now.

The lieutenant radioed back that it couldn't be done with the force he had, not without significant air support softening up the defenses. But the weather precluded that, and was expected to stay problematic for several days. Jenkins could hear the conviction in the lieutenant's voice—it was like the sound of a chisel grating against metal.

The general wasn't interested in what the lieutenant had to say. Generals were careerists. That's how they got to be generals. Military officers were like any other professional—they were ambitious and had personal agendas, often more so. This general had made a decision that this particular hilltop had to be taken on that day. With the resources currently available. Why? What for? Nobody fucking knew. Generals didn't explain themselves.

Jenkins heard the chisel sound in the lieutenant's voice again when he radioed once more very firmly that it was "not possible. Repeat, not possible." He was at the site and could directly assess the situation based on the hard reality in front of him. The captain with Jenkins was well inside the parameters of the fortified base and hadn't been out on more than a few missions. And the general—the thought of him sitting out there on that ship was enough to make Jenkins feel like the top of his head was going to blow off.

Jenkins stepped way outside the bounds of protocol and said to the captain, "Sir, the lieutenant's right. They can't do it. The map indicates it's a pile of rock in the middle of nowhere. It doesn't matter. Not even a little bit. They can't do it."

The next time Jenkins saw the lieutenant, who had led his men in a disastrous failed attack, he was being medivacked out in a Huey, with no rib cage on his right side. As Jenkins and the captain watched the helicopter rise, Jenkins gave the captain a look that no enlisted men should ever give an officer. Three days later, he was transferred to supply operations with no explanation. If they'd specified a reason, most likely it would have been mental instability, and then they would have had to give him a discharge, which was a reward the army was extremely loathe to hand out to an insubordinate grunt.

Jenkins heard Timmy come back into the apartment a bit later. She came out onto the balcony and asked for a sip of his beer. They sat in silence.

"So, who are you, Roy Jenkins?" she asked eventually.

He looked out into the night. "Couldn't really tell you. Questions like that are more up Jack's alley. I go where life pushes me and deal with it. I don't try to figure things out so much. Don't know if life can be figured out. If it can, it ain't gonna be me that cracks it."

"You ever wish your life was different?"

"Different?" He wondered what she was asking. Whether she was asking herself rather than him.

"When I was a kid running around the streets of Shadyside," he said, "one of the shittiest neighborhoods in Pittsburgh, I never once thought about my future. I never thought about what my life was gonna be like or what I was gonna do with it. The kids I knew were just kids. They were wherever they were, never thought about being someplace else, never thought ahead. We just did stuff. Threw rocks through windows, stole cars to go joyriding, shoplifted shit. Walked around a lot. Sat on swings in the asphalt parks, no grass. I hung out with different bunches of dead-end kids. We lived in the moment." He massaged his eagle tattoo.

"Choices always seemed like a luxury to me. Life just happens to you. That's the way I see it.

"I'll admit, there were a few times I got the feeling there were things going on out there I didn't know about. But I figured maybe they weren't for me, and left it at that.

"A guy like Jack, you said it, he has it all and blows it. Stupid. Maybe if I'd had a few things going for me, I'd have done something else with my life. But I've always been a firm believer that what could have happened did. And I can live with that. I can live with the hand I've been dealt, do it with 'equanimity.' That's a word I learned from Jack—means evenness of mind. Not a lot of people can say that, even among the folks with advantages."

Timmy leaned over and kissed him on the lips. He hadn't seen it coming, not even a little, and didn't react. She kissed him again. He responded. She slid her tongue between his lips. They stood, and Jenkins pressed his thick, muscled body against her thin frame, which felt much firmer than it looked. She leaned back a little and looked at him, ran her fingertips lightly over the shallow pockmarks on his face, over his mustache. The wind had picked up—it might mean a *meltemi* was coming, the powerful warm summer winds occurring some years in the western Mediterranean. The crickets were silent.

He pulled her T-shirt over her head, unbuttoned her cutoff jeans. His touch between her legs quickly made her wet. She unzipped his pants and found him hard. He lifted her onto the railing, and she put her hands on his hips, pulled him to her. He resisted, entering her very gradually. She moved her hands to his buttocks and pulled harder. He filled her. She wrapped her legs around him, and together they plunged into a pool of carnal sensation, cloaked in darkness.

CHAPTER 11

Somehow, Jenkins had led them around the bodyguard posted behind the villa. The guy had to be nearby, probably not more than a hundred yards away. Jack imagined him bored out of his mind by nothing happening for hours on end and his job's seeming lack of necessity. The guard must be aware that virtually nobody knew where the big man was. Maybe he'd even dozed off for a while, as Jack had done earlier.

* * *

Sleeping arrangements in the apartment changed. Jack found his stuff neatly arranged on the couch. He was surprised but okay with it. Timmy and Jenkins hooking up relieved him of whatever miniscule responsibility he felt for her, and breathed fresh life into their dying triumvirate, which he was still clinging to like a lifesaver ring in a raging sea. For her part, Timmy was a little bit stung that he adjusted so readily, but knew she shouldn't be surprised and felt a comparable relief as well.

Two mornings later, Jack sat by himself at a table in the back row of the Oasis, perusing a three-day-old *Tribune* he'd found on an empty table. On the lower right of page three, a headline seized his attention. His heart started pounding:

178

IDI AMIN'S WHEREABOUTS STILL UNKNOWN

AP Associated Press

July 15, 1989

MANAMA, BAHRAIN. Exiled Ugandan dictator Idi Amin has dropped out of sight since leaving his home in Saudi Arabia three weeks ago and was rumored to be in Zaire, Arab diplomatic sources said Friday. The sources said on the condition of anonymity that they believed Amin had travelled to Kinshasa, the capital of Zaire. They had no information on reports that he left there for the Saudi port of Jiddah on Wednesday.

The former Ugandan leader has lived in Saudi Arabia since his overthrow in 1979.

Amin, 61, arrived in Zaire on a false passport. He was expelled to Dakar, Senegal. From there, he was expected to return to Saudi Arabia, but has not been on passenger lists for any flights to Saudi Arabia since.

A Saudi diplomat said Saudi officials were angry with Amin for leaving the country on forged documents and had refused him re-entry into the country. He said the former dictator has long been unpopular with his Saudi hosts for meddling in African politics and for his links with Ugandans opposed to the current government there. In past phone calls from Jiddah to The Associated Press Bureau in Bahrain, Amin made it clear he hoped to recapture power with the help of supporters and relatives in Uganda.

Amin was ousted from his East African nation in April 1979 and was granted political asylum in Saudi Arabia in 1980 after the Libyan government of Col. Moammar Gadhafi refused to harbor him.

During eight years of tyranny, tens of thousands of Amin's political opponents were killed, and newspaper reports alleged he practiced cannibalism. The reports were never independently verified.

Saudi businessmen acquainted with Amin said they had no idea of his whereabouts but insisted he has not returned to Saudi Arabia.

Saudi officials could not be reached for comment.

"Idi Amin's whereabouts are becoming a mystery. Officials are being tight-lipped," said a Jiddah hotel manager who said Amin used to visit him regularly. The hotel manager said Amin left Jiddah with two other men, and that his second wife and 22 of his children still were in their guarded villa halfway between Jiddah airport and the city.

After initially racing through the article, Jack read it again slowly, word for word, and then again.

Holy fuck. So, that's who it is. Rafe referred to "the big black bugger" and mentioned "Zaire" and "the Saudis."

What an unbelievable fluke that he'd seen the article. It seemed like an omen.

———————

Jack couldn't find Jenkins all day. *The bastard must be out playing at being a fisherman.*

Early evening came and he scurried to the Kentavros.

Thank God, Jenkins was there, on his stool. "Bette Davis Eyes" was playing loudly over the bar's sound system. Jack's insides were jangling, and he paused a few moments inside the door to collect himself. He listened to the music. Massively overplayed a few years back, the track still sounded amazing. "She's precocious. She knows just what it takes to make a pro blush." The music bed throbbed with rich textures, and the gritty female voice ached with feeling.

He sat down next to Jenkins without either of them greeting the other, not unusual for them, though there may have been some residual tension from the after-dinner unpleasantness. He and Jenkins hadn't interacted since then. Jack ordered Johnny Walker on the rocks—for no particular reason, he'd recently switched from Dewar's. They sat there, not saying anything.

Jack leaned over to Jenkins and whispered in his ear, "I know who it is."

Jenkins turned and looked at him directly, something he rarely did. "Yeah? What is it you think you know?"

Jack leaned close to Jenkins again and said almost inaudibly, "Idi Amin."

Jenkins tried not to react, but his expression gave it away. A look came over his face that Jack hadn't seen before. He couldn't tell what it meant. They resumed their silence, now charged with tension.

"Let's go for a walk," Jack said, knowing that if Jenkins was going to discuss this at all, it wasn't going to be with other people around.

Jenkins finished the remaining half of his beer in one long drink, which Jack took as assent and downed his whiskey. They left and headed up an inclined street away from the busier parts of town. They made no conversation. Jack couldn't get a read from Jenkins, which in some ways was more unsettling than if Jenkins had been glowing with anger. It felt like Jenkins had shifted into a new mode, though Jack didn't know what.

They came to the small plaza in front of the blue-domed church, empty and quiet. Sat on the church steps. Jenkins seemed tired, but again it was hard to read him.

Jack took the article from his jeans pocket and presented it.

Jenkins seemed to relax a little when he saw the headline. He read slowly, using his finger a few times.

"This doesn't say shit."

"It doesn't say shit except to someone who heard Rafe. I heard him refer to stuff in the article. I know it's him."

"Yeah, so?"

"So, I know it goes against everything in you, and you don't owe me a goddamn thing. But I'm asking you to tell me what island he's on? And before you answer, think about this—you *can* tell me. You *can* open your mouth and make the sounds. It's physically possible. The world won't come crashing to a halt. You can say it out loud. It's just the name of a place."

Jenkins sat there, apparently lost in thought, though maybe he was just letting his mind go slack.

Jack pressed on. "If you tell me, it won't mean anything. I'm nobody. I can't do anything. Come on, Jenkins. Please."

Jenkins stunned him by saying, "Capsis."

Jack was at a loss for words. It hadn't occurred to him that Jenkins would just come out with it easily. He'd been prepared for a long back and forth, maybe a series of them at different times in different places, conducted carefully, strategically, in which the slightest misstep on his part could shut down the dialogue.

He shrugged inwardly. *Who the hell knows why people do what they do? They don't even know themselves half the time. Whatever, he told me which island it is.*

Proceeding carefully, acutely aware the situation still had a precarious balance, he said, "Never heard of it. Where is it?"

"It's a private island. One villa only. Near Skiandos, about forty knots southwest of here."

"What's he doing there?"

"Same thing he's always doing. Trying to stir up support to regain power. The guy's completely nuts. Doesn't have a chance in hell, but he keeps trying. After the washout in Kinshasa, and with the Saudis royally pissed off at him and refusing to allow him back in, he got in touch with his Swiss banker. He still has plenty of money there. Looted the hell out Uganda when he was in power. The bank arranged for the rental of the island. According to Rafe, the villa is known in certain circles for privacy and discretion at a premium price. So, for now, he's operating from there. He's out of his mind."

More snatches of the conversation Jack had heard through the port-holes made sense now.

Why'd he tell me where Amin is so easily? The question kept popping back into Jack's head. And he wasn't coming up with an answer. *He probably figures the tidbit of info won't put me in a position to do anything. And that I wouldn't have the balls to do anything even so. He doesn't know I know about his guns. He thinks I'm all talk. Which is probably true.*

"You know, it's not as crazy as it sounds," Jack said carefully. "Baby Doc's been living in a luxury villa in the south of France since he was overthrown a few years back. Apparently he has an unwritten agreement with the French government that he can stay there as long as he doesn't interfere in Haitian politics. I read he has his meals delivered from a famous three-star restaurant nearby. The goddamn US Air Force actually delivered him to France in one of their planes, one of the many examples of America's blind fear of communism driving it to support evil leaders. Baby Doc was one of the most corrupt of all time. He stole something like five hundred million dollars from his country. And he lived the life of an international playboy while his people were dirt-poor, living in incredibly squalid conditions. Thousands of people were tortured and killed under his regime.

"It's supposed to be a similar deal with Amin in Saudi Arabia. He's supposed to stay out of African politics, but it sounds like he isn't sticking with his end of the bargain. Doesn't know when to leave well enough alone."

Jack heaved a sigh, feeling drained. For a few moments, he almost felt a sense of ease sitting there with Jenkins in the peaceful little square. The church bells began to chime.

"It's crazy the way the world works," he reflected. "You become a tyrant dictator and torture and kill thousands, ruin a country. And you wind up living in the lap of luxury in a rich country, protected and keeping a good chunk of the money you stole. How does shit like that happen? It's so completely wrong. Amin should have been torn limb from limb back in Uganda when he was overthrown. From what I read, his getaway helicopter lifted off minutes before his people got their hands on him. And now he's here in Greece on a private island, plotting his return to power."

He started to say more about that but decided not. Let things settle.

"How did Rafe hear about it?" he asked.

"Amin's looking for people to make a move with, and Rafe's one of the people you contact when you want to do something like that. Or used to be. Amin's out of touch. Rafe wasn't interested. Knows Amin doesn't have a chance. Knows the man's bat-shit crazy. Funny thing is, right after the contact, he heard through other channels of a price on Amin's head. Maybe someone's taking the guy seriously. Rafe found that proposition more appealing. Amin tortured a friend of Rafe's once. Amin never made the connection to Rafe. But assassination is dangerous work. And Rafe considers himself retired. He's done soldiering. It's a hard way to make a living. He's got a sweet life now in the south of Spain, along with all the other villains. They all pat themselves on the back for having made it to their place in the sun, though some of 'em made some unpleasant stops along the way. Besides, for Rafe, there's easier ways to make money these days, like what I'm doing for him."

"Why did he tell you?"

"He likes to show he's still in on stuff. Rafe likes to impress, to be a big man."

From this point forward, the only thing Jack could focus on was taking things to the next level. His mind was in hyper-drive every waking moment, zeroed in as never before. Later that same night, he was at a bar by himself drinking, and the ghost people hovered behind him and hissed incessantly in his ear, "Guns, guns, guns." Those were the first words he'd heard them speak.

They were right. He needed Jenkins' guns. He could maybe steal them and leave the island immediately, but he had no idea how to use them. He'd only ever fired a .22 rifle in his life, in the woods near his house as a kid. Besides, an undertaking like this needed a lot more than just guns. A lot of things would need to be figured out. It called for planning, preparation, foresight. His brain reeled from the dozens of questions bouncing around inside his head. Could he do this? How would he get there? How would he do it? *What do I need besides guns? A boat. Map. Water, food. A compass.* He felt foolish, like the time he ran away from home when he was eight, filling a pillowcase with what he absurdly thought were essentials, like an iron skillet and peanut butter and jelly. It embarrassed him to think of himself as an innocent child, before he'd warped and twisted into the creature he was now.

This is ludicrous. I'm being just like the Walter Mitty idiots I ridicule all the time, sitting around trying to figure out how I'm going to pull off an adventure. Is it even remotely realistic to think I could do this? Seems doubtful since I can't even figure out all the things I need to think about. He scratched the scar on his knee and considered taking a swig from his flask, but the bartender was staring at him. *I probably look a bit crazed,* he thought.

Jenkins could figure out how to do something like this. I've got to convince him to sell me his guns. Show me how to use them. Otherwise, I won't even get out of the starting gate. I might as well try to get his guidance for the rest of it, too. There's nothing to lose by trying.

The next morning, after Timmy went out in a cheery mood, Jack, in what he hoped came off as a casual way, sauntered out onto the balcony where Jenkins was having his coffee. He had no idea where to begin. The task of trying to persuade Jenkins to sell him his guns was beyond daunting. It made him feel like he was about to try swimming upriver through whitewater rapids, something that simply wasn't possible for any human.

"Listen," he blurted out, "I know you got guns. I looked in your duffel." He was scared of saying this but had no choice.

Jenkins' eyes narrowed; he looked sideways at Jack. "Yeah. I thought so."

"I'm really sorry," Jack rushed on. "I shouldn't have invaded your privacy like that. It was wrong." His apology sounded like the rattle of a hollow gourd. "But compared to what I'm about to ask you, it's not going to seem like that big a deal."

Jack looked at Jenkins' face that conveyed nothing.

"Listen, I want to buy your guns," Jack skipped ahead so as to get to his point, though it didn't seem like Jenkins was about to interrupt. "Amin is a bad guy. As bad as they come." Jack's words hung in the sunny morning air, didn't seem as if they remotely had the weight they needed. But Jack forged on, stepping up his rhetoric. "He's evil incarnate. He's trying to get back in power, and should be stopped. He tortured and killed tens of thousands of people, for no good reason, sometimes for just not being from his tribe. And he's supposed to have *eaten* one of his wives. He forced all the Ugandans of Asian descent to leave the country with only what they could carry—over a hundred thousand people forced out of the country where most of them had lived all their lives. He destroyed Uganda. Everyone there lived in terror of his insane deadly mood swings. He filled the rivers with dead bodies. His people hated him. He should have been killed when he was overthrown. Justice should have been done then. Assassinating him now will just be serving up justice deserved long ago. Not to mention the sick injustice of a monster like him living in luxury now off all the money he stole from his country. Killing him is the right thing to do. I wouldn't be so absurd as to suggest I have morals, but I am saying morality is on my side. Completely."

This was the first time either of them had referred to killing Amin. Jack had avoided it because it felt as if saying it out loud would reveal how blatantly preposterous the idea was. But it couldn't stay unsaid any longer.

Jenkins calmly sipped his coffee, smoked his cigarette, and gazed out at the landscape. As if Jack weren't even there.

"Come on, you were a soldier." Jack got ahead of himself.

Jenkins spoke up at last. "Don't see what that has to do with anything." He scratched his stomach. "Like I told you, I never saw any action. I'm not who you think I am. I don't know why I'm even bothering to tell you all this, but listen carefully. I've done odd jobs all my life, some of which involved violence. The army set me up in the munitions business for a while, and I still do some transport now and then. I've worked as a bodyguard, as security, and a bouncer, the bottom of the barrel job for guys like me. Eventually, I lucked into some construction work and wound up with some overseas jobs. But that's it. I don't know about assassinating people."

"But you can figure out how to do it a thousand times better than I can," said Jack. "You've had training. You know how to use guns. You've been around war. You've been around people who know how to do things like this." Jack took a breath. "And you're you. I'm a dead-end loser. I need you to tell me how to do this. I'm begging you, please. This is my chance. My one shot. I've got to take it. It's too perfect to pass up. It's so much in the right. And it's such an extraordinary fluke that it crossed my path. I've got to do it."

Jenkins sipped his coffee. The birds chirped, cicadas hummed.

"Come on, please, one man to another. I can't figure this out by myself. You've got to give me some help. Some guidance."

"I don't got to give you shit," Jenkins said, anger bursting out. "And my guns? Are you out of your fucking mind? Do you actually think I would let you have my guns? To do something as bat-shit as this?"

"I don't expect you to understand," Jack kept on. "But this is what I've wanted all my life. To do something really exciting that matters and is the right thing to do. I can't get my excitement from doing bad stuff, like robbing banks. I'm not saying I care all that much about right and wrong, but getting my excitement from doing something bad just won't work for me. I've got to do something that's right. And this is the most completely right thing I'm ever going to come across. And it just fell in my lap. I feel like I'm meant to do this.

"I don't want to do bullshit thrill seeking anymore. I want to do something that's. . . that's important. Something that all right-thinking people will know is good. And I don't give a damn how stupid or crazy it seems.

"Think about when the Israelis kidnapped Eichmann and smuggled him out of Argentina. Yeah, sure, they kidnapped him and broke about a dozen international laws, but who cared? Every sane person in the world knew they'd done the right thing, which had to be done to achieve any semblance of justice. And the right-thinking world applauded them. Eichmann got a tiny piece of what he deserved, and fuck the Argentines who complained. They welcomed the Nazis into their country with their plundered wealth and thought it was fine.

"Killing Amin is like capturing Eichmann. Amin escaped when he should have been killed. Justice can be done now." He cleared his throat.

"I've been waiting all my life for something like this. And now I've stumbled on it by a gargantuan coincidence. It's mind-boggling—the circumstances coming together that made this even a possibility. And it's right here, right now. I can't pass it up. I've got to try. Can't you see?"

"You'll get yourself killed," said Jenkins. "Not that I give a shit. The world will probably be a better place without you."

"Maybe I will. Let's say probably. I'm willing to chance it. I'm willing to risk getting killed in order to try this. Think about that. And it's not as if my death will matter to anyone. I'd actually be doing a big favor for everyone I'll otherwise meet down the road. And if I actually kill Amin, I'll be doing the world a big goddamn favor.

"Maybe I'm insane. Maybe I'm not all that different from the guy who shot John Lennon or the nut in the Austin bell tower or the chick who didn't like Mondays, but at least I'm trying to steer my lunacy in the direction of something right, instead of evil like all those people. I'm trying to channel my insanity in the direction of good.

"Are you getting any of what I'm saying?" Jack glared at Jenkins as much as he dared. He went inside and returned several moments later, drinking from a container of orange juice.

"I'm a complete asshole, I know it. I'm fucked up in the head. I'm leading a terrible life, treating people like shit, doing nobody any good. I went down the wrong road a long time ago, and I'm not ever going to get it right. I am who I am. All I want to do is this one good thing, which has come my way by a series of coincidences that boggle the mind. They make it seem like destiny. I'm begging you, please. Help me.

"I'm at the end of my rope. I can't keep living the way I live, and I can't find another way. I feel desperation every minute of every day, and not the quiet kind either. Can't you see? There's no . . . no relief for me. I have to try this. It's a fluke on top of a fluke on top of a fluke. I'm going to try it one way or another. Even if I have to try to sneak up on him with a steak knife."

With no sense it was coming, no welling up of sadness inside him, Jack suddenly began to cry. He was as surprised as Jenkins. It was literally the first time in years. He sobbed and gasped for breath. Leaned over the railing, pushing his hips against the top bar till it hurt. Tears fell to the dirt below, and soon long strands of mucus dangled and broke.

Jenkins got up and walked out of the apartment.

CHAPTER 12

There was no reason at all for Jack to be surprised, but as he looked through the trees, he was astounded by the sight of the massive, dark brown man dressed only in billowy lime-green swim trunks, sitting casually in a straight-back chair with arms, relaxed and smiling. For some odd reason, it struck Jack that the hovering aerial witness created by his mind should place an emphasis on the term "trunks" when it came time to describe the scene for posterity. Amin was a large man indeed.

* * *

Jack woke the morning after his crying bout, sensing movement in the room. Groggy, he raised his head from the uncomfortable foldout bed and saw Jenkins sitting at the table having coffee. Jack got out of bed and shuffled over to the kitchen area. He could see that Timmy wasn't in the bedroom or bathroom, and figured she must have had an early shift. He took a box of cereal and a bowl from the cabinet, poured some cornflakes, opened the fridge, and found there was no milk.

"Fuck," he exploded, throwing the bowl across the room against the wall, shattering it and sending cereal and ceramic pieces everywhere. He laid his pained head down on the counter and rested it there. "Let me buy your guns off you," he moaned. "I'll pay you way more than they're worth. You can always get more." He straightened up.

Jenkins gave his paunch its morning scratch. "Can you get your hands on five thousand for the rifle and two thousand for the pistol?"

"Yeah. It'd take me a few days, but I can do it."

Jenkins drank some coffee and yawned. "I ain't selling you my guns."

"Why not?"

"Don't want your money."

"It's as good as anybody's."

"Maybe. Though now that you mention it, maybe not."

Jack lost control. He stepped over to the table and leaned across it, putting his face a foot or so from Jenkins', and shouted, "Listen, you numb-skulled moron. I'm going to kill Idi Amin or die trying. He's scum. He deserves to be wiped off the face of the earth. He's guilty of crimes against humanity. No different than gassing the Jews. And you're toying with me about selling me your guns. It's bullshit."

Jack didn't even see it happen. Jenkins snatched him by the throat and stood in the same motion, knocking over the table and his coffee. He backpedaled Jack fast across the room, shards and cornflakes crunching beneath their bare feet, and slammed him against the wall near where the cereal bowl had hit.

Jack's eyes bulged out, and his face turned bright red. He was stunned by how strong Jenkins' grip was, didn't think he could get it loose if he tried.

"I don't have to help you do a fucking thing, you little shit. Not one fucking thing. You're a spoiled junkie who's going down the drain fast.

You don't give a fuck about right and wrong. You've never had to cope with real life. So don't tell me what I got to do. You've got no idea what people got to do."

Jenkins tightened his grip further, and Jack struggled for air. His eyes showed wild panic. He could feel his brain being deprived of oxygen and realized he was going to pass out and might never regain consciousness, depending on when Jenkins let go.

Jenkins released his grip, and Jack dropped to his knees, coughing harshly, gasping for breath.

"So, he's a bad fucking guy," Jenkins muttered to himself. "I get it."

Late that night, Jack wound up in a randomly selected, dark vestibule somewhere in town, with his tongue heatedly mashing against the tongue of a black woman he'd met in a club about twenty minutes earlier, who was American but lived in Munich and had truly magnificent breasts, while her older German boyfriend was outside in the street calling her name repeatedly, which later on Jack couldn't remember for the life of him. She undid his jeans and took his cock out and stroked it a few times; he almost came. But then she slipped from his arms and hurried outside before her absence became too much even for a boyfriend who wanted to believe whatever bullshit story she was going to sling. Jack stood in the dark hallway, his semi-hard dick sticking out in the night air. He doubted if sex would have relieved his anguish anyway.

Later that night, he leaned back against a wall in a narrow alley and gradually slid down to a sitting position, then tipped over in slow motion onto his left side. Lying in that position, he made a supreme mental effort to find something good inside himself that was of his essence, something good that was part of his true self. But all he could feel inside was the seething storm of large quantities of methamphetamine and whiskey. He tried to cry again, but his tear ducts had gone dry.

The next morning, Jenkins woke Jack early from a dead sleep and signaled him not to make noise and get dressed. The bedroom door was closed, and Timmy was likely still sleeping. They left the apartment, with Jenkins carrying his duffel over his shoulder. For a brief moment, Jack thought maybe Jenkins was leaving for good without saying goodbye to Timmy, but that didn't make any sense, and on a second glance the duffel didn't look anywhere near full.

Jack didn't ask any questions as Jenkins led the way to one of the many shops renting motor scooters, open at dawn to receive returns from people departing on the early morning ferry. He told Jack to rent a 150cc.

After the rental procedure, Jenkins got on the bike and started the engine, and motioned for Jack to get on behind him with the duffel. Jack could feel the hard, heavy objects inside the thick canvas. They rode out of town and along the southern coast; there was almost no traffic.

As they neared the end of the island, Jenkins turned right onto a dirt trail leading into a pine forest. Jack had passed the trail every time he'd gone to Banana beach, but it had never registered on him. After a dozen bumpy minutes, they came to a meadow of wild grass three or four feet high. At the far end of the field was a stone barn halfway fallen down. No other signs of civilization.

Jenkins took out the guns and ammo, and assembled the rifle.

"To be on the safe side," he said, "I figure we'll need to get out of here within twenty minutes after we start shooting in case someone hears and comes looking. Doubtful, but it'd be dumb to take a chance. So, we're gonna make the most of our time, and shooting practice will come last.

"This here is an M16. It's an automatic rifle, meaning it shoots continuously when the trigger is depressed. There are thirty bullets in each magazine, but it's best to shoot in short bursts, both to correct your aim if needed and to avoid jamming. I've got ten magazines. Each bullet can do severe damage to a person if it hits a vital spot.

"And this here is a Browning semiautomatic." He picked up the handgun. "Meaning you shoot once by compressing the trigger, and the gun automatically puts another bullet into the chamber, but it won't shoot again until you compress the trigger. You need to release the trigger after each shot. It will *not* shoot continuously if you hold the trigger down. The Browning has a thirteen-round magazine, and I've got ten of those too.

"This morning you're going to use one magazine of each for practice. Are you listening?" he snapped at Jack, who was looking dazed and overwhelmed.

"Yeah, I'm listening." He shook himself and made an effort to focus and concentrate.

"One of the most important things about shooting a gun and hitting what you're aiming at is to be prepared for the recoil and control it. Both these guns have medium recoil and you should be able to handle it after you get a feel for them. For the Browning, hold the wrist of your shooting hand firmly with your other hand to steady it, like this. Everything about shooting a gun should be done in a firm, steady, but relaxed way. I'm going to say that about a hundred different ways until it sinks in, so get used to it. The Browning recoil is going to cause the muzzle to lift, so the best thing to do until you get the hang of it is to aim a little low. And squeeze steady. Jerky movements make you miss. Aim with one eye closed. And use the sights. They're there for a reason—they make for greater accuracy than just pointing. Don't let panic or rushing cause you to shoot without using the sight. Take the extra moment. Using your sight significantly increases your chances of hitting your target, along with staying as calm as possible. And of course getting as close as you can, the biggest factor of all."

He picked up the rifle. "With the M16, you have to make absolutely sure the stock is lodged tightly against the front of your shoulder whenever you're firing, like this. Both for steadiness and to keep from breaking your shoulder. Again, nothing should be done with too much tension. Everything should be done firm but relaxed. And you squeeze the trigger. Don't pull. Squeeze. When the magazine is empty, you pull it off like this"—he removed it with a loud click—"and put the next one on like this"—he reinserted it with a snapping sound.

"Before we fire a single round, we're going to go over all this until I'm satisfied you got it. If it takes an hour, then we'll take an hour. Whatever practice we do, it's not gonna be anywhere near enough."

Jack went through the motions of using the guns again and again, with Jenkins repeatedly telling him to breathe and relax. He must've said a dozen times that the failure to hit something close was almost always the result of panic, rushing, and fear, all wrapped up together. "It's actually not that hard to hit something at close range if you stay calm and don't rush."

This was a new version of Jenkins, one that Jack had sensed was there, and he was glad he turned out to be right. He was somewhat awestruck by Jenkins' familiarity with the guns and even more his focused business-like manner. He'd hoped for something along these lines but wasn't prepared for the actuality of it. At one point, he almost laughed out loud at the meticulous capability Jenkins was displaying so matter-of-factly.

Jenkins finally allowed him to shoot. The target was a hand-drawn X on a piece of paper tacked to a tree about fifteen yards away. He shot with the Browning first. His first shot, which missed, sent a strong rush of adrenaline surging through him. Firing a real handgun felt nothing like he'd repeatedly imagined it. Some of the difference was the heft of the weapon, and there was the kick as well. And as Jack was belatedly realizing, reality was just plain different than the imagined.

Firing bursts from the rifle was even more satisfying, more visceral.

He hit the paper three times with the Browning and nine times with the M16, all nine in his last fifteen shots.

Jenkins didn't seem satisfied but said it was time to leave. They cleared out quickly and didn't pass anybody on the trail.

Jack didn't try to discuss with Jenkins anything about their practice session. He could feel that whatever Jenkins was doing, his willingness was delicately balanced and could easily tip backward. Whatever decision Jenkins had made, Jack sensed it was far from being set in stone.

It didn't feel like he'd made the determination in his head, but rather in his gut. Though that didn't seem exactly right, either. All Jack knew was he strongly didn't want to break the spell.

The second time they went for training, Jenkins brought a map, which he spread out on the ground, and they kneeled to look at it. It showed Kyros and Skiandos, both with only one town, built around a harbor, and a sparsely populated countryside. The much smaller Capsis was about six knots northwest of Skiandos, in the direction of Kyros. Capsis looked like a person could walk around it in about two hours, maybe a bit more. It had a prominent headland at the southern end with a small bay on either side, which seemed like a prime position for a villa, but the house wasn't shown on the map.

"Okay, listen," said Jenkins. "Skiandos has regular ferry service and no airport, just like here. But I don't think you should travel to Skiandos and launch from there. In an island village, they'll take note of a new arrival, especially if you're around for a couple of days preparing. And you don't know the island. You'll fumble around asking questions, attract attention. Getting a boat could be tricky, too. Renting one will mark you for sure. And stealing one could be a disaster, especially since locals tend to keep an eye on things, and you don't know people's routines there.

"My idea is I get a boat for you here on Kyros. I can get one with a ten-horsepower outboard. Since it won't be returned, you're gonna have to give me cash up-front to cover the cost of a new boat, plus fifty percent extra for the owner's trouble. I'll let you know how much. You should be able to get to Capsis from here in about three hours. You'll need some food and plenty of water. And you'll need a disguise for the attack, at least a mask, and a change of clothes, so they won't have an accurate description of you afterward. You're going to need a good pair of binoculars for reconnaissance. And a knife. I'll give you mine. A compass. Electrical tape. A flashlight. You can have my canteen, too. Make a list of everything you'll need, and make sure you have every single item. If you can't get something, talk to me.

"At the villa, there's gonna be bodyguards. How many we don't know, but the most it'll be is a half dozen, probably less. You're not going to kill all of them, and they're going to have a high-speed boat gassed up at their dock. If you try to get away in your little putt-putt, you're not gonna get far. So, I'll get a second boat here, a small rowboat, no engine. We'll have to make sure the oarlocks are well greased. The oarlocks on the motorboat, too. Same money arrangement for the rowboat.

"After you sight the island, stay a good distance away and go around it, see where the villa is, what kind of cover there is. Get the lay of the land and whatever else you can figure out. Use the binoculars carefully. The last thing you want is a bodyguard catching a reflection and thinking somebody's scoping the house. Your only hope is gonna be catching them completely by surprise.

"After you locate the villa, stay well offshore and go along the coast until you find a place where you can put in without being seen from the villa or the grounds around it. Row the motorboat in—don't use the motor—and find a cove if you can. There, you transfer everything you won't need on Capsis to the rowboat. Then you walk the rowboat along the shore away from the house and find another cove, hopefully one where you can hide it completely. Cover it with branches so it can't be seen unless you're right on top of it. Cut them with the knife. Don't snap any branches, no matter how far you are from the villa.

"Are you getting all this?" he said with irritation.

Jack nodded grimly.

"You go back to the motorboat and use electrical tape to fix the motor firmly in position so the boat will go straight in the direction you point it, and get strips of tape ready to fix the throttle at full. Put some heavy rocks in the bottom of the boat so it won't ride too high." He took a long swig from a water bottle and wiped his mustache.

"You're gonna make your attempt in the early evening if you can. If you don't get yourself killed and you manage to get to the motorboat, you start it and send it due west without you in it. I'll make sure the engine starts on the first try. Then you get to the rowboat as fast and quiet as you can. Hide there as completely as possible. Don't move around at all. Get under some cover and stay still.

"They're probably gonna hear your motorboat leave, and they're gonna go after it in their high-powered boat. They'll search the island, too, either right away or when they get back from finding your motorboat with nothing but rocks in it. You'll probably have to stay motionless and well hidden for hours, absolutely quiet. But it'll get dark before too long, which'll be exactly what you'll need. They may use searchlights to keep looking for you after sundown. You stay put till you're sure they've given up for the night. It could be midnight or even later.

"Then, you very quietly row to Skiandos. It should take you about three hours. Use the compass to point yourself in the right direction—southeast forty-five degrees. Do you know how a compass shows forty-five degrees southeast?"

Jack nodded.

"Check the compass every ten minutes. As soon as you're in deep water, dump the guns and extra ammo in the water.

"When you get to Skiandos, find a place to land where there's some cover. Away from houses or where there might be people around, but not too far from town if you can. Hide the boat as best you can, so it's less likely to be found right away, but don't get too hung up on that. Walk into town and catch the first ferry out, going anywhere. Check for people watching who's boarding. Try to attach yourself to a girl or a group. You're good at that. Stay calm, act normal. If Amin is dead, the Greek authorities will get involved at some point, but it might not happen right away. There probably won't be police there, but just in case, have a story prepared about your stay on Skiandos—the name of the place you stayed. Look at your guidebook. And a couple of places you went while you were there—a beach, a café—so you can bullshit someone, even though your story won't hold up if it's checked. You're just trying to talk your way onto the ferry.

"Once you're on the ferry, make friends if you haven't already. As the boat arrives wherever it's going, go up top and look for people watching the boat come in. Get off with your new friends. And again, be relaxed, act normal.

"If there's no problem at that point, take the next ferry or plane going anywhere else. And keep going until you get to New York, even if you weren't planning on going there. Lose yourself there.

"Now, repeat everything I just said."

Jack was in a state of complete overload. He felt stunned. He couldn't believe Jenkins had thought of all this, knew to think about all of it. Detail after detail. He felt like he was drowning. And he was rapidly losing faith in his ability to do this.

On his sixth try, he described the plans to Jenkins' exasperated satisfaction.

They had a quick shooting practice. Jack hit the target with six of thirteen shots and twenty-two of thirty.

As they got ready to leave, Jenkins said, "Next time, we're gonna talk about the hard part, doing the deed. We don't have enough info to plan it with much precision. You're gonna have to make some judgment calls after you get to the island and see what's what. You ain't gonna be able to count on anything going as planned anyway. Everything can go to hell in a second. Like I said before, that's when you're gonna find out who you really are, Jackie boy."

As the training progressed, Jenkins barked and growled at Jack constantly. Ordered him around, verbally abused him like a drill sergeant, repeatedly calling him "stupid" and "pathetic." He seemed to be in one continuous foul mood, but Jack sensed something else was going on with him too, though he couldn't think of what it might be. Jack figured it was his imagination, but for one of the few times in recent weeks, he felt his intuition was functioning properly.

A pit had formed in Jack's stomach between the first and the second training sessions, and didn't go away. Morning, noon, and night, it gnawed away. He thought he might be getting an ulcer and popped antacid tablets by the handful, never one to skimp on pills.

———————————

Back in town, the two of them talked even less than before. Jack used his willpower, such as it was, to make sure he didn't subject Jenkins to rants and diatribes during this time. He didn't want to take any chance of derailing him.

Timmy knew something was up. Something was different, weird. She left it alone for a while, thinking it had to do with the shift in relationships. She and Jenkins spent time together, just the two of them—dining out on her evenings off. They had a favorite taverna they usually went to, up on a hillside in the village, overlooking the harbor. When they arrived, they were usually warmly welcomed at the street entrance by the owner, who led them through the humble interior to emerge onto an elevated garden with a magical view of the bay at night. Off to the left, the harbor-front restaurants and cafés had strands of decorative lights outlining their awnings, some glowing warm ivory, others multicolored like Christmas lights. The garden terrace was covered by trellises with vines and purple bougainvillea spread over them, and had other flowers planted in random spots—vivid red, sunny yellow, a pale pink. The place had a slightly touristy feel, but it struck a pleasing chord for Timmy and Jenkins. He discovered he liked freshly caught octopus seared on the restaurant's outdoor grill, and ordered it every time. The owner knew of him from the fishermen, and Timmy, with minimal effort before going out, was the type of customer every taverna on the island wanted to seat in a prominent place.

It was strange for Jenkins to be with a woman as beautiful as Timmy. He didn't feel quite ogre-like, but not far from it. There was the noticeable age difference as well. For her part, though, Timmy always took his arm as they walked together, and gave off unqualified pride in her man.

Jenkins borrowed a motorboat one day and drove her around the island, showing her its full splendor from the remove of the sea. They found a little beach surrounded by cliffs, reachable only by boat. They had it all to themselves and swam nude, another first for Jenkins. He found it felt great to lie naked on the warm sand and dry in the sun without a wet bathing suit. He thought about how to describe the feeling, and settled on the word "free."

Timmy had never in the past been drawn to brawny men, but with Jenkins the physicality came with a solidity of person, a quality she hadn't focused on before but now found quite appealing. A term she'd never used came to mind when she thought of him: a stand-up guy.

"What's up with you and Jack?" she eventually asked him one night over dinner. "Is it you and me being together? Or did something else happen between you guys?"

Jenkins was evasive, and in her usual way she didn't press the matter. A part of her had a vague sense she might not like the answer.

She did ask, "Where do you guys disappear to in the mornings sometimes?"

"I talked him into trying fishing with me. With poles, not nets. Convinced him it would be good for his head, give him some relief from his crazy ways."

"Jack fishing? That'd be something to see."

The explanation didn't hold water in about a half-dozen different ways, but it was what he came up with. He didn't like lying to her, but never doubted it had to be done.

One evening Jack and Jenkins were at the Kentavros without Timmy, and Jenkins said very simply to Jack, "You know, you're gonna get yourself killed."

Jack almost said "Yeah" with false bravado, but at the last moment changed his response to "Maybe."

Jack gave Jenkins cash for the owner of the boats. Jenkins hated not returning them, and wasn't looking forward to the conversation.

In a flippant moment, Jack said to Jenkins, "I'm going to be famous."

"Most likely, nobody's ever gonna know this even happened."

They went for more training sessions. Jenkins mapped out an elaborate practice area to simulate the whole plan. He designated a place for the attempt, another place about three hundred yards away where the motorboat would be, though the actual distance would be farther, and a third spot another hundred yards along where the rowboat would be hidden. He had to make a lot of assumptions about how the house was situated, the layout of the grounds, possible cover, and the direction from which Jack would find it best to approach. He had Jack go through the motions of approaching the target area, entering it, aiming and shooting, and then running for cover, downhill to the sea, along the shore to the motorboat, and finally the rowboat.

"Like I said, you're gonna try to make your attempt in the early evening, when it's half light out," said Jenkins. "You're gonna have to do it when he's outside. There's no way you're gonna get him inside the house, so don't even think about it. There'll be a pool. Maybe the big man likes to swim. And people here spend lots of time outdoors, have meals outside.

"If he doesn't come outside on the evening you arrive, you'll have to wait for the next one, sleep on the island. Worse comes to worst, you might have to go for it at some other time of day, which'll hurt your chances of getting away, but I don't think it'll come to that. People here usually come outside for some part of the evening.

"Like I said about five dozen times already, your only chance of pulling this off is catching 'em completely off guard. And getting close. *You gotta get close.*

"Virtually nobody knows Amin is there, so the guards are gonna be sitting around with nothing happening all day and all night. Even the most professional bodyguard eventually turns off his state of high alert.

"The whole thing is gonna happen in all of about fifteen seconds, if that. You'll have to figure out an approach where you can get within fifteen feet of Amin before you have to start shooting. You've practiced at fifteen yards, so fifteen or twenty feet should give you a pretty good chance of hitting him. I'm guessing you'll either approach the villa from tree cover or from lower ground where the rise will give you cover. Once you get as close as you can still hidden by cover, you put your disguise on and take your safeties off. *Do not forget: take—your—safeties—off.*

"You wait until a moment when Amin is exposed, meaning there aren't any obstacles between you and him. Once there's a moment like that, you go. Don't wait for it to happen again.

"Try to shut down your thinking. Just focus on the actions that are part of the plan. If you think too much, you'll fuck it up. At any given moment, just focus on your next few moves. Have your first three steps fixed in your head before you go in, and make a mental note of where the guard is who's closest to you. Once you're in the midst of it, just go with how we practice it. Let your muscle memory guide you.

"You're gonna hold the M16 down by your side like this. The Browning should be tucked in your waist like this, on your left side, grip forward, so you can grab it easily.

"You walk toward them quickly. Don't run. Running will alert them right away something's wrong. Walk steady but quick, and you'll buy extra seconds while they wonder who the fuck you are and what the fuck you're doing there. You're not gonna look like an assassin. You do this right and you should be able to shoot Amin before they react. Focus on him and stay calm. *Look only at him. Don't look around.* Raise the M16 into position against your shoulder, aim with your sight at the middle of his chest, and fire a good burst. If you miss, re-aim and fire another. If he goes down on the first try, shoot the guard nearest you, then run like hell. Don't try to get more than one guard. They're gonna react fast if they're any good, which they almost definitely will be.

"If it takes two tries to get Amin, forget about the guards and just run like hell. If you don't get Amin in two tries, then you ain't gonna get him, and get the fuck out of there.

"Run directly away from them until you reach cover. Then turn downhill to the sea and haul ass. Watch where you place your feet so you don't twist an ankle or take a spill. When you get to the water, run along the shoreline to the motorboat. Unless the guards are close behind you, don't even think about stopping and trying to take them on. You won't stand a chance against more than one experienced shooter. When you get to the boat, start the engine. Like I said, I'll make sure it starts. Point the boat due west and give it a shove.

"Then quiet as you can, move down the shore to where the rowboat is. And hide there for the rest of the evening without making a sound. Move as little as possible. Barely breathe."

By this point, Jack knew he couldn't do it. It was impossible. What had he been thinking? It was too overwhelming. There was too much to keep track of, too many things to do, too much of everything. There were *way* too many ways to fuck up. He simply didn't have the capabilities or the gumption, not even close. In his ridiculous life, he didn't do complicated things. He was smart but had little experience with being disciplined or diligent, in forcing his mind to stay locked in, avoid mistakes. Those were abilities people acquired by trial and error, by doing things and making mistakes and learning to maintain focus in order to avoid them the next time. It just wasn't possible he was going to be able do all this without making major mistakes. Fatal mistakes. Standing there with Jenkins, he suddenly found himself struggling to get his breath.

He'd never understood how complicated this was going to be. He couldn't believe Jenkins was able to foresee the whole thing, how it would unfold, could anticipate so many elements, even if it was a lot of guesswork. How was he able to figure all this out? In such detail? *He must've done something like this before*, Jack thought. *He must've at least been in some shooting situations, even though he denies it. Rafe implied as much.*

Standing near the mock motorboat position, he started to tell Jenkins he couldn't do it, that Jenkins should just stop talking. But as the words were about to come out, he vomited violently, his body heaving and spasming, then limply twitching. When two heaves in a row came up dry, Jenkins, without giving him a chance to say anything, told him to repeat everything he'd just said.

Jack stared at the gunk on the ground. He noticed some yellow pieces in the goop and wondered what they were. Still bent over, hands on his knees, overcome with reluctance, he slowly repeated what Jenkins had said as best he could, with numerous mistakes and lapses. Jenkins made him do it four more times until he got it straight. Then made him do a walk-through of the plan, shouting directions at him each step of the way. After Jack did that three times with diminishing guidance, Jenkins had him run full speed for the running parts, and walk carefully and quietly for the other segments.

Jack couldn't understand why Jenkins was still bothering. It was clear to him beyond any shadow of a doubt that he couldn't do this. There wasn't a hope in hell. He'd crumble into tiny pieces, completely shut down, or just freeze entirely.

He assumed Jenkins knew this, which made him wonder all the more why Jenkins was continuing, why he was still bothering to put him through his paces. But Jenkins showed no signs of relenting. Like an actor refusing to break part, he went on as if Jack were actually capable, as if he were actually going to attempt it. He made him do the full course five more times, correcting mistakes, reminding him of things like breathing, which Jack kept forgetting to do.

Maybe he's waiting for me to admit I can't do it, thought Jack. His brain was muddled and exhausted. *Maybe he wants to force me to say it out loud.* Jack was on the verge of screaming it at least a dozen times, the words forming on his tongue. But Jenkins' command over him somehow prevailed, and the words didn't come out. Jack was amazed he held it together until the end of the session.

On the back of the motorcycle, racing back to town along the coast, Jack felt delirious and jelly-like, wildly disoriented.

Back in town, he became extremely listless. In his head, he'd given up. He wasn't going to do it. It was completely clear. He was just waiting for Jenkins to tell him it was off.

———————

Jack couldn't find decent binoculars for sale in town. So he went to a few of the nicer hotels and strolled around their pools and private beach areas until he saw a pair lying unattended on a lounge chair. He sauntered by, casually picked them up, and kept walking. The guidebook lying next to them was in German, which made him feel less bad about the theft. The binoculars were high quality—Nikon, strong magnification, sharp focus.

In a tchotchke shop, he found a Zorro mask and a girl's wig that was a bright shade of red, perfect as part of a Halloween costume. In a tackle shop, he bought a compass and checked that it gave accurate readings.

He'd lost all the passion that had roared out of him the morning he'd aggressively demanded Jenkins' help. He merely went through the motions each day. Jenkins gave no sign he noticed the changes in him. Timmy figured his life was finally catching up with him and he was having some kind of breakdown. He didn't resemble the hipster asshole she'd originally met, didn't carry himself in the same way. He seemed to be in a daze all the time. He slept a shocking amount. She asked Jenkins if he thought Jack was coming undone in a way that was more than the usual mess he was.

"Yeah, he's getting his come-uppance. It was bound to happen sooner or later. It's probably for the best."

"What's going on? Not that I care that much, but he seems like he's worse off than ever. Like he might need professional help."

"I'll deal with it," said Jenkins.

Sunday was the easiest day for Jenkins to get use of the boats. On the Friday morning before the fateful day, Jack finally realized Jenkins wasn't going to tell him he couldn't do it, wasn't going to tell him not to go. It just came to him—Jenkins wasn't going to stop him, save him. It was clear. As to why it was up to Jenkins and he had no say, it was as if his will had been drained from him, and Jenkins had somehow taken control. He didn't know how or when it had happened. Jenkins had never seemed like the type who could dominate him. Maybe he himself had changed, become more pliant, weakened by his massive abuse of self. He felt agitation and foreboding all the time. And cowardice. Raw, gaping gutlessness. Like there was an octopus-like tumor of dread inside him, wrapping itself around his organs, making him sicker with each passing day.

Earlier in the week, he'd gone out for a couple of nights of unbridled debauchery, consisting more or less of feverish hysteria, as strange as it was to feel anything resembling fever in the unbearable heat. He got ferociously high and frenzied on his sacred methamphetamine. Danced like a demon. People steered clear of him, and he avoided human contact. He was alone in his own private typhoon.

The shadow people were his constant companions. He spoke to them, told them about nightmarish visions he had—a Cambodian man with a deformed arm standing at the back of a stall in a crowded *souk* beckoning him to come behind a curtain the man held open; a little red-haired girl with exceptionally white skin wearing a white summer dress, whose face became monstrous when he moved closer to her; running across an African savannah at his absolute fastest speed, with a full-grown lion loping behind, easily catching up with him and bounding heavily onto his shoulders, taking him down; seeing a man on a small-town street dressed in a drab gray suit and somehow knowing he was a thrill-killer and was going to murder that night, and when he tried to shout out an alarm, no sound came from his mouth. The shadow people understood it all. They nodded sagely.

Early on Saturday morning, after he'd been out all night, just as the sun was first breaking the horizon, he stood on the silent, empty promenade, and it came to him that he was wrong about not being able to do this. He *was* able to do this. He was *going* to do it. It was his time, his moment.

He'd probably die. He had an intense fear of being tortured, especially by a man who enjoyed it and who he'd just tried to kill. He knew he'd squeal like a pig being sliced up alive. He would beg and plead and scream, all to no avail. He imagined what it would be like to know that nothing he could say or do would stop the unbearable pain he was somehow bearing. He knelt down on the pavement facing the emerging sun blazing in the distance and took a sacred oath to force himself, if it looked like he was going to be caught, to put the muzzle of the Browning to the roof of his mouth and pull the trigger. He'd have to anticipate things carefully to make sure there was no chance of getting away but not wait until it was too late.

During the day on Saturday, he had periods of strange calm. He carefully made a waterproof packet containing his remaining supply of speed, split up into separate doses, plus a number of cutoff straws. When the time came for valor, he would fortify himself with the white powder, which should make him feel powerful and more capable. Maybe enable him to focus more intently and hold it together better under what was sure to be a shit storm of panic and terror.

CHAPTER 13

The blood. The shocking crimson curling through the air in slow motion. Misshapen blobs separating from twisting, elongating streams. And the mist. The red mist.

* * *

Sunday morning, before sunrise. The boats were moored to a rickety dock in a small, secluded bay about three-quarters of a mile outside of town, in the direction away from the coast with all the beaches and hotels. All the things they'd need were already stowed onboard, except the weapons and ammunition. Jack had actually slept, fitfully, but he'd gotten some rest.

The two men walked silently along the dirt road, a little before six. The chirping of birds filled the air, which didn't seem right to Jack with doom filling the atmosphere around them. Didn't birds have a special sense of a storm coming?

Jenkins carried his duffel containing the weapons and ammo. Jack's knapsack was slung over his shoulder, and in it was a change of clothes, his passport, wallet, and a toothbrush, which seemed silly under the circumstances. He also carried a plastic bag containing a dozen oranges and a half dozen bars of dark chocolate. His waterproof packet of speed was in the buttoned lower pocket of his cargo shorts, where there would be the least chance of it falling out. He wasn't as full of dismay as he'd expected. Extremely shaky, yes, but resigned.

The ghost people trailed about ten feet behind, making no sound. Not the shuffle of feet, or rustle of cloth, or sounds of breathing. It occurred to Jack that they probably didn't need to breathe.

Jenkins and he arrived at the dock, built low over the water, a couple of slats broken, one missing. They walked out and stood next to the boats. Turned to one another and looked squarely in each other's face for several moments, something they'd never done before. Neither said a thing. Jack untied the boats, got into the back of the motorboat, and secured the line from the rowboat. He pulled the starter rope on the outboard motor, expecting a roar to rupture the silence, but the engine produced only a loud purr modestly disturbing the morning hush.

Jack was in equal parts surprised and not surprised when Jenkins climbed into the back of the motorboat and nodded firmly at him to move forward.

They headed out to sea, slowly at first, Jenkins' hand on the tiller. Somehow they'd both known it was going to be this way.

The wind picked up when they got away from land. The waves were mid-sized with whitecaps. Jenkins checked the compass every so often, and Jack sat up front getting wet. He thought about the indomitable power of the sea. In his gut, a feeling of toughness intermingled with the frailty that lingered from the last several days. He took his flask from his back pocket and had a swig; he'd already done a morning line. During his recent days and nights of chaos and breakdown, it had occurred to him that maybe his hatred of life and people wasn't as total and unequivocal as he'd thought. No doubt about it, he was a bad person, but maybe not quite as vile as he thought. In the course of his life, he'd found deep, almost mystical pleasure from beautiful and wondrous things, which probably didn't count for much, but it might mean his insides weren't pure ugliness.

Dread began to permeate his entire being, head to toe. At the same time, though, he felt an almost electric charge of being dynamically alive. He'd learned well over the years what gave him a feeling of vitality, and he'd been right about this endeavor. Rising up through his sense of foreboding and calming him somewhat was a sense of exaltation. For a few moments, as they bounced roughly over the waves, he experienced something akin to rapture.

It was indeed three hours when Capsis became a speck in the distance. They went a bit closer and then circled it slowly, far offshore. They were lucky. Unlike a lot of Greek islands, Capsis wasn't predominantly bare rock. Pine forest and other foliage covered large parts of it. Almost as helpful, the terrain was hilly and uneven. Three quarters of the way around, they saw a large white villa at the base of the headland.

They studied it with the binoculars, and after Jenkins was satisfied, continued around the island, still well offshore, until they found a place not too far from the house where they could row to shore unseen.

"We should put in around three," Jenkins said. "That'll give us time to reconnoiter before evening. There are a lot of variables, and there's definitely gonna be some things we didn't predict. We'll have to see what the story is, adapt as needed.

"I'm going to use the M16. I'll target Amin."

It was the only thing that made sense now that Jenkins was bringing his skills to the attempt. Jack felt a massive sense of relief, even more than when Jenkins got in the boat. Jack getting the full experience he sought wasn't even a distant consideration.

"You'll have the Browning and go for the bodyguard nearest us. If we both get our man, we'll try to shoot any other guards nearby. There's two of us, and if we're lucky we might get Amin and two guards. Then we run like hell. If serious return fire starts before we get everybody we want, we turn tail sooner, regardless of who we've hit, including Amin."

The boat rocked gently in the waves, and they settled in to wait in the merciless heat, relieved occasionally by Aegean breezes. They ate oranges and chocolate, drank plenty of water.

The time came and they rowed in. The greased oarlocks muffled the sounds almost completely. They found a fair-sized inlet and entered it.

They prepared the motorboat for later—pointed it outward, fixed the engine in position, tore strips of tape to have ready to secure the throttle at full. Selected a half dozen sizeable rocks from the shallow water and carefully placed them in the bottom of the motorboat, making a minimum of noise, though the small sounds they did make rubbed roughly on Jack's raw nerves.

They transferred to the rowboat all the items they wouldn't need on Capsis—compass, flashlight, knapsack, all but one of the plastic bottles of water, and the food except two oranges and two chocolate bars. Jenkins made sure Jack kept two extra clips of ammo in one of his pockets and that he jammed the wig and mask into another. They pulled the rowboat along the shore away from the villa. They found a perfect cove, surrounded by thick vegetation, the entrance obscured by trees, Jenkins cut branches and covered the boat completely. Jack took a last swig from his flask and reluctantly stuffed it into his knapsack in the rowboat.

They returned to the first cove, and Jenkins told Jack to wait there, he'd be back in about an hour. Taking only the binoculars, with the knife strapped to his leg and canteen on his belt, he headed inland, uphill.

A heavy drowsiness came over Jack. He lay down on a bed of pine needles, which felt amazingly comfortable, and, though it didn't seem possible, he dozed off.

He woke when Jenkins jostled his shoulder.

"He's there. I saw him swimming. He's a big bastard. They have one guard on the high ground behind the house with an automatic rifle. Looks like a Heckler."

I don't give a damn what make it is, thought Jack.

"There were still two guards on the terrace, like we saw from the boat. One with an automatic rifle, the other with a machine pistol. There may be more. I don't know. I didn't see Amin with a weapon, but his reputation is he likes to carry a sidearm, pearl handle, according to Rafe. He's s'posed to be very attached to his military roots. Rafe says he got his military training from the English."

That definitely goes in the "no good deed goes unpunished" file, thought Jack.

"On this side of the house," Jenkins continued, "there are stairs going down the bluff to a beach. We could go up the stairs unseen from the house, but if someone looks over, we'd be completely out in the open. And it looks like when we got to the top, the pool would be between us and the terrace, the most likely place for him to be if he's not in the pool. It'd be great to catch him swimming, but that's unlikely.

"On the far side of the villa, though, the approach is flat and there's trees up to about thirty feet from the pool area. So that's gonna be our approach.

"There's a table and chairs on the terrace. The woman hangs out at the pool all the time. She looks like a pro."

They each ate an orange and a chocolate bar, drank deeply from the water bottle, and topped up the canteen with what was left. Jack did some speed. He got jittery, had trouble sitting still. Got the urge to gab but managed to restrain himself.

"After we move out," Jenkins said, "we talk only when we have to, and we whisper close to the other guy's ear. Use hand signals if possible. Watch where you step and keep all sounds to an absolute minimum. If the guards hear anything that makes them nervous, they're gonna get a lot more alert, and our chances will pretty much disappear."

At six-thirty, Jenkins stood up, M16 in his hands, binoculars hanging from his neck. Said, "Let's go."

In his head, Jack wasn't ready, not that he ever could have been. *That's it?* he thought. *There's got to be something more.*

Jenkins was already headed uphill. Jack followed lifelessly.

They made their way up a slope of open, rocky ground. Jenkins had told Jack to stay about ten feet behind. The heat was brutal. An incessant cacophony of cicadas buzzed all around them, maddening but masking their minor noises.

Jenkins stepped carefully, his manner exuding focus and concentration. The back of his shirt had a wide sweat stain running down the middle. Jack's clothing was drenched and his pores leaked steadily. About two thirds of the way up the hill, Jenkins signaled they should turn right, in the direction of the villa. Jack guessed it was about half a mile away.

For some reason, he looked back down at the sparkling Aegean stretching out to the horizon, only one distant island breaking up the amazing blue. He thought of how he'd dreamed about it as a teen. Thought of its soul-stirring beauty, and for an instant wondered whether he should abandon the maniacal venture at this late juncture. He was sure the right answer was yes, but kept going.

A few minutes later, he was hit by the full impact that he could have never done this on his own, not even close. The thought of him trying to do this by himself was a sad, grotesque joke. His brain would have melted down by now, and he'd probably be curled up in a ball on the ground, hugging his knees, being the sniveling sack of shit he was. If he somehow made it to the villa, it was certain a farce-like catastrophe would ensue. Even with Jenkins along and taking charge, he had almost no faith in how he was going to handle himself when the time came. He'd felt nauseous on and off all day, and now the queasiness seemed to have settled in for the duration. He hoped it didn't reach the point of heaving, if for no other reason than the noise.

They entered a pine grove where the sound of their steps was muted. Angled uphill. Jack wondered where the guard posted behind the house was positioned. Jenkins moved more slowly, stopping often and listening.

Sunbeams filtered through the trees, idyllic and beautiful, contrasting sharply with Jack's sensation of floating in a nightmare. Rivulets of sweat trickled steadily down his neck and below his armpits. He yearned for a cool, high-pressure shower beating on his scalp, washing away all the grit and stickiness. He was breathing heavily, struggling for air, more than just the result of physical exertion. He craved more speed but held off.

They stopped a few feet short of the edge of the pine thicket, and Jack could see the corner of a terra-cotta roof several hundred yards away. The rest of the villa was hidden by a thick stand of trees at the base of the promontory stretching out into the sea. There was a small bay down to the right with a pretty sand beach, and Jack could see the stairs leading up the bluff. All the ground between where they stood and the stairs was rocky and open. Jack would've felt horribly naked and exposed had they approached that way.

Jenkins signaled to head uphill again, staying inside the tree line. They hiked about fifty yards more and came to a ridge top, which looked to be the high point of the island, running along its spine. Jenkins led them quickly over it, bent low, and down the other side about twenty feet. They turned right and trekked parallel to the ridge for about fifteen minutes, long enough to pass behind the villa and more. There was no path, and dense branches consistently blocked their way, which they had to carefully bend or duck under to avoid making noise. Jenkins repeatedly put his finger to his lips.

They sat down on a fallen tree trunk and rested, their breathing returning closer to normal. Then they trudged back up to the crest and ducked low again as they quickly crossed over. A pine forest covered the long, downward slope in front of them, and Jack saw through the trees, far below, about half of the bright white villa. The pines were Mediterranean and thus without branches for the first thirty or forty feet, where a thick canopy spread out overhead. The effect was church-like, which seemed oddly appropriate. They walked slowly downhill, on full alert, conscious of every sound, both of their own making and otherwise. The carpet of pine needles was a gift from the gods. They came upon a weathered board nailed high on a tree trunk with the words "The Waiting Room" painted on it in faded red against a white background. After several moments of confusion, Jack remembered where he knew it from and felt an infinitesimal speck of amusement, despite feeling quite ill. He had a momentary urge to explain the sign to Jenkins but knew he wouldn't have the slightest interest, and it wasn't worth the whispering. Jack wondered whether it was a good omen or a bad one. The novel was one of his favorites, but the hospitality served up at the fictional Villa Bourani had been a decidedly mixed bag.

As they got closer, the barometric pressure ratcheted up a few notches. Jack's agitation was peaking, and his nerve totally abandoning him. Some kind of breakdown was happening inside him. He felt wobbly. His body's messaging systems overloaded, short-circuited. He felt confused, wasn't entirely sure what was going on. He was once more having trouble catching his breath. He saw shadow people hiding behind trees everywhere he looked, but they were in gray uniforms instead of their usual robes.

He slumped to the ground, wanting to just think for a minute, collect himself. But Jenkins grabbed him by his arm, pulled him to his feet, and gripped his head with both hands, one on either side, like a clamp. Put his stony face close to Jack's, and shook his head forcefully. "Snap out of it," he whispered fiercely. Jabbed his chin downhill in the direction of the repugnant villa. Feeling beaten, Jack resumed his shuffle downhill, with Jenkins right behind him. Jack wanted more than anything to lie down and go to sleep again, as impossible as it would be to lose consciousness.

He didn't care about killing Amin anymore. Not in the slightest. He didn't care about having a real-life adventure or living life to the full or this being his one shot. Or his moronic ideas about the pursuit of being interested and benevolent terrorism. Or any of the rest of his repertoire of wild bullshit. He didn't feel the thrill of excitement, just thick cables of tension and panic stretching inside him to the breaking point, and when they snapped, he was sure he was going to shatter into a million little pieces.

This is unbearable. I can't stand another moment of it. I've got to get out of myself, escape this feeling. He had a vision of his lifeless sack of skin crumpled on the forest floor, as his slug-like corpus of flesh and bones crawled away.

How is Jenkins doing this? Is he some kind of android? He just keeps going. Like he's possessed. Like I was. It's as if all the need to do this gushed out of me and poured into him. But that would mean there was something unreal at work, and I'm not that far gone. He is executing my harebrained scheme, though, and is somehow able to maintain control of himself. Why's he's doing it? He'd had some guesses back on Kyros. *What were they?* He couldn't bring them to mind.

He threw up without any sensation it was coming. Immediately covered his mouth and held the viscous goop in his mouth and his cupped hands as best he could, making a supreme effort to muffle any gurgling. Jenkins moved quickly to his side, put his mouth to his ear, and whispered, "Don't make a fucking sound."

Somehow Jack managed to quash the gagging and retching. Put his face close to the ground and carefully let the muck pour out. Sat down, and Jenkins allowed it. Jack wiped his hands on the ground and then his shorts.

Jenkins again put his mouth to his ear and whispered almost inaudibly, "Remember, Amin is a bad guy. He deserves to die. Take your safety off."

Jack did as told. And put the bright red wig on and the Zorro mask, not feeling the least bit silly, as bizarre as the scene must have appeared to the aerial observer who in the last several moments had materialized in the air above them. Jack knew he was hovering there as a witness, projected by his brain, though he seemed completely real, floating up there gazing down.

Jenkins took out a stretchy black cap and pulled it over his face. Two large holes had been cut out for his eyes.

They reached the side of the villa without further incident and stopped behind by a wall of cypress trees, which, as Jenkins had said, were about thirty feet short of the terrace and the spacious pool. Jenkins had somehow guided them completely around the bodyguard behind the house, though he couldn't be far away.

Jack peered through the dense foliage and, though it made no sense, couldn't believe what he saw—Idi Amin sitting at a table with a top made of blue and yellow ceramic tiles, wearing elephantine, bright green swim trunks. It was as if it was the last thing in the world he expected to see. Like the visual elements were being projected as far as the surfaces of his eyes but were blocked from entering his brain.

Amin held a tall glass filled with ice cubes and clear liquid, and was talking in a relaxed way with two men in street clothes seated on either side of him. Jack wondered if Amin's beverage was alcoholic. He had some vague notion that Amin was Muslim, though from what he understood Amin's gargantuan ego was pretty much the sole arbiter of his personal conduct. The cicadas had quieted down, but their sound still grated Jack. It was like blood rushing in his ears. At least it was a white noise obscuring the sound of him and Jenkins breathing, which sounded to Jack like the loud sucking of air.

The woman strolled out of the house still wearing only the garish purple bikini bottom. The men took no notice. She dove into the pool, swam to the far end and rested her arms on the ledge, then swam to the ladder and climbed out. Turned a lounge chair to face the setting sun and laid down, her large breasts pointing upward to the sapphire sky. *How'd she wind up in this situation?* Jack wondered. *Life is so astoundingly weird. People too, the queer creatures we all are but like to pretend not to be.*

He felt Jenkins' lips brush against his ear and whisper so softly Jack had to strain to hear. "The guy to Amin's left has a rifle lying on the terrace next to him. The guy on the right has a machine pistol holstered. Amin doesn't have any weapon I can see. You go for the guy with the rifle. If we both get our targets, we try to shoot the other guard. Then we run, hopefully before anybody else shows up. Maybe we'll get lucky.

"I'm gonna count to three with my fingers. Then we start walking. Fast and steady. Grab your shooting wrist with your other hand so you're ready."

Jack did as told but almost screamed out loud, "No-o-o-o." *This can't be it*, his brain shouted in passionate protest.

Jenkins raised his left hand, holding the rifle in his right, and with emphasis raised one finger, two fingers, three.

Jack felt Jenkins' hand on his right shoulder propel him forward, and they pushed through the dense branches. For a fleeting instant, Jack's mind went blank, but he quickly focused on the guard with the rifle lying next to him, trying to block everything else out. As he reached the beginning of the flagstones, he raised the Browning and aimed. He heard a burst from Jenkins' rifle and a howl of pain. Out of the corner of his eye, he glimpsed Amin's large body flying over the table, which turned over with a crash, and at the same time he fired at the guard. His chair went over, but he was immediately scrambling, reaching for his rifle. *I missed. Shit.* Jack heard another burst from Jenkins. He pointed his pistol again, tried to use the sight, and pulled the trigger. The guard grunted and winced. He heard a deep voice bellow from behind the overturned table, "SHOOT THEM! SHOOT THEM!" A short burst came from where he sensed Jenkins was.

Jack's guard, wounded or not, rose to a kneeling position, his rifle came up, and Jack watched in horror as he fired in Jenkins' direction, a long, continuous burst that seemed to reverberate endlessly. Jack's attention was yanked to where the guard's rifle was pointed, and things went into ultra-slow motion, the visuals seeming to stall and float. He saw Jenkins' chest explode with blood, streams of shocking red spurting out and hanging in the air.

He turned and ran like a maniac. He knew he was sprinting at his absolute highest speed, but it seemed like it was taking forever to reach the wall of cypresses for which he felt the most profound love. He heard a burst of fire behind him and felt a biting pain on his right shoulder.

He rammed through the mass of foliage and continued straight for maybe fifty yards, then took a sharp right and hurtled downhill toward the sea. The ground was rocky and uneven, and he was acutely aware of being out in the open. He kept a wary eye on where he planted his feet.

He got to the water. Heard yelling up the hill behind him, but nothing nearby. He turned right and splashed frantically along the shoreline, forced to run in the shallow water because of thick underbrush growing right up to the water's edge. His left foot landed on a submerged rock, which gave way and his ankle rolled on its side, with a sharp stab of pain. *FUCK!* He kept running, knowing a sprained ankle didn't usually disable you right away. The unable-to-put-your-weight-on-it kind of pain showed up a few hours later, along with the bulbous swelling.

He got to the motorboat and walked it out of the cove. When the water reached his thighs, he pointed the boat in a westerly direction and pulled the engine cord. It started, as Jenkins had promised. Jack gripped the back of the boat, taped the throttle at full, and the boat jumped out of his hand.

He limped back to shore and hobbled quickly, as quietly and with as much vigilance as he could manage, inside the trees lining the rocky shore. Partway to the rowboat, he heard the roar of a big engine from across the island. The hunt had begun.

CHAPTER 14

Jack became aware of his right shoulder throbbing with pain. Between his crazed desire to get away and single-minded concentration on following the instructions Jenkins had drummed into him, he'd forgotten about his injury. With the chaos and adrenaline, the pain hadn't made its way into the conscious part of his brain. He turned his head and raised his right arm slightly to get a look at the wound. There seemed to be a groove in the outside of his shoulder about a half inch deep and two inches long, though there was so much blood it was hard to tell. Fortunately, the vital fluid was oozing rather than flowing at this point, and he guessed he didn't have to worry about bleeding out. He'd been extraordinarily lucky. A couple of inches to the left and the wound would have been much more disabling, much less bearable. He knew the pain was going to get worse, and infection was a serious concern.

He took a clean pair of underwear from his knapsack and pressed it hard against the gash for five minutes, timing it with his Swatch. The oozing seemed to stop. He put his hands in the saltwater and rubbed his palms together vigorously, cleaning them as best he could. He carefully splashed saltwater over the gouge repeatedly, and used the remaining electrical tape to fix a clean sock over it. The process worsened the pain considerably, and he was gritting his teeth by the end.

He lay down on the ground a few feet from the boat, under some bushes, and strained to hear sounds in the woods. He decided to do some speed and with a shock realized he'd completely forgotten to do the massive fortifying blast right before the attack as he'd planned. *Fuck! If I'd done the blast, I might have performed like I should have. I'd have believed in myself. I might have been capable. Fuck, fuck, fuck. How could I forget? Jenkins might still be alive.*

He checked his packet. The waterproofing had worked. He hadn't allowed the thought to enter his mind that water might have leaked in when he'd walked the motorboat out to sea. He opened it and did two large bumps.

From the moment he'd begun to run, he'd been so focused on getting away, he hadn't thought about the cataclysm the attempt had turned into. Now he forced himself to think back and re-create the god-awful mess. The gruesome image of Jenkins' chest bursting open with strands of scarlet floating in the air was seared in his brain. He knew immediately there would be no getting rid of it. It would be in his head as long as he lived. He didn't deserve to ever be free of it.

The catastrophe was completely his fault in every sense. His Armageddon. He'd come up with the deluded idea, had been the sole driving force. He'd worked Jenkins over relentlessly to get his guns and his help. He'd knowingly used Jenkins' anger and animosity to manipulate him, get him to come around. He'd even managed to break down sobbing for the first time in his adult life. Had no idea how he'd managed that.

When he'd first walked up to Jenkins in the bar in Athens, his intent was to enlist his help to do violence. He'd failed, but within a short two and a half months he'd managed to get Jenkins to go along with an infinitely more difficult and hazardous assault. It seemed like from the first time he laid eyes on him and sensed the violence there, he'd been scheming to draw him into his twisted vision. *Was that really true? Had it all been about that?*

When it came to the crucial moment, he'd failed pathetically, with mind-boggling incompetence. He'd gotten two shots off at the guard. Missed once entirely, and while the second had wounded the guard, it failed to put him out of action. Panic, fear, ineptitude had all seized him in their fiery grip, had ruled him. The guard recovered and fired his appalling blast. He was a pro and did what he was supposed to do. Unlike Jack, the bungler, the imposter. The mammoth hoax. As full of self-loathing as he was, he still had trouble grasping how colossal his fuck-up was.

He'd gotten Jenkins killed. He'd found out who he really was, just like Jenkins said: a gutless loser who didn't have the strength of character to pull off what he'd been seeking for most of his life. The verdict fit him with cutting precision, scalded like a branding iron pressed to his flesh.

Jack remembered catching a flash of the other guard sprawled awkwardly on the terrace. Jenkins must've shot him. But based on the yelling, Amin hadn't been killed. Maybe wounded. Probably. He'd seemed to soar over the table as Jenkins started shooting.

I got Jenkins killed. My out-of-control wants, my utter lack of the stuff it takes to be a man.

It was harder than I thought. Fear and panic, the blur of everything. It was insanity to think I could do it. I got a good man killed.

I liked him. As much as I ever liked anybody. And I got him killed because I wanted some fucking excitement, adventure. As if it was just some experience you have, like climbing a mountain. But it wasn't. It was going into combat to kill a man protected by armed guards, something that required real backbone.

It doesn't matter at all about morality or justice being on my side. Not in the least. Jenkins was living his life. He was doing fine. It wasn't his fight, his need.

I really thought we were going to pull it off, or at least he was. I thought he was invincible. But it all went to hell in the fraction of a second.

He heard the sound of the powerboat moving across the sea with loud thumps. He wondered how long it would take them to find the motorboat. And what they would think when they found the rocks in the bottom? He heard sounds of movement in the woods, but nothing nearby.

It got to be nine o'clock, dusk in the Aegean in August. The full cloak of night would soon follow. Jack couldn't stop thinking about Jenkins. His gut told him that the outcome meant his world-view was wrong, had always been wrong. In the most fundamental ways. How he viewed life, people, human endeavor. He didn't know what he was supposed to do with this knowledge. Would it make him different? Could knowing something change a person? His way of being was so entrenched. He was still a young man, though he felt very old. He probably had more than a few years left, probably decades, if he truly wanted to see if somewhere inside his putrid self there was a new way of being.

He felt a paralyzing sadness, dug his fingers into the dirt he lay on. He'd done wrong, not right. This shouldn't have happened.

He wanted Jenkins to be alive, to be with him now. That was the way it was supposed to be. Jenkins not being there seemed metaphysically wrong, whatever that meant.

The powerboat returned and circled the island twice, shining powerful lights in every direction. Jack knew he was too well hidden to see but kept perfectly still anyway, barely breathing.

———————

Around midnight, he tried to stand and fell over in the shallow water. His sprained ankle wouldn't take more than a small amount of weight. His shoulder felt as if someone was digging a hot knife into it. One last time, he listened intently for any human-made sounds coming from the island or the sea. None. He crawled over the gunwale. Put the oars in the water, checked the compass. And as quietly as possible, pushed the boat out and began to row. As with everything else Jenkins had promised, the oarlocks were well-greased and almost noiseless.

Even as he strained to be quiet, it was disconcerting how many sounds you made when you were determined to make none. But he felt strangely confident that his small noises weren't carrying far, and there was the steady concealing slap of waves. The night was dark—a quarter moon, partly cloudy sky, only a few stars showing to the north.

He dumped the guns and ammo. Checked the compass every five minutes or so. Quickly got blisters on both hands from rowing. Wrapped spare clothing around them, and kept going. Wondered how far a walk it would be to the ferry and how he was going to make it with his ankle. He'd find a way, he knew.

He wondered where Amin was, whether he was wounded, how badly. Who he thought had tried to assassinate him. The crazy red wig and mask. Jack had pulled them off and stuffed them in his waistband early in his mad dash. Buried them in the dirt where the rowboat had been hidden.

He thought how he really hadn't turned out to be so different than the self-indulgent idiots in Germany and Italy who played at being terrorists, dishing out mayhem and death for no apparent reason other than boredom, anger, and excitement. He wondered whether humans were supposed to escape boredom. Clearly, it was a natural part of life that most people dealt with without major turmoil or distress. *What's wrong with me? Why don't I work right?*

He wondered how broken he was, how unbalanced. Not as an excuse, just to know. The shadow people were nowhere around. *Will they show up again?*

The knowledge he was going to run out of speed soon filled him with a sense of desolation. He could feel the creepy, despicable creature he would turn into then.

He calculated he had roughly enough left to get him as far as some fleabag hotel in Athens. It was going to be an interminable flight to New York without the drug. He did a small bump. He'd do a serious blast when he got ashore, which should help him push through the pain and get him onto the ferry.

The thing he'd been trying to avoid thinking about was why Jenkins had decided to join him, but the question loomed in the mist in front of him. Along with that, when Jenkins had made the decision?

Why does anyone do anything? he thought. *Because life presents them with a decision, and they make it . . . And sometimes they make a bad one.*

Jack knew he'd never know the answers. He wasn't a person who could ever fully understand someone like Jenkins.

Did Jenkins leave the cash for the boat owner? What happened to the woman? Did she watch it all happen? What went through her mind? Jack's head began to fog and drift.

He became aware of a feeling that was completely unfamiliar to him. He turned it over in his mind, examined it, used all his mental faculties to detect what it was. After several long moments, he realized it was shame. Deep reprehensible shame. Abiding.

The darkness began to lift and he could see the outline of Skiandos several hundred yards away. He was going to make it that far at least.

Timmy woke up, surprised to find them gone. She figured they'd be back mid-morning like the other times. Her mood was light and airy. She was looking forward to Jenkins walking through the door and looking at her the way he did, making her feel warm inside. She'd been thinking it was time for the two of them to move on without Jack. Or maybe Jack would move on, and they'd stay.

She lazily started preparations for a hearty breakfast when they returned.

www.ingramcontent.com/pod-product-compliance
Lightning Source LLC
Chambersburg PA
CBHW071501170626
46811CB00007B/2665